Always There For You

Halli Starling

Halli Starling Books

Contents

Representation and Content Warnings

Representation

- Amelia (she/they) is white and demisexual. She also suffers from a chronic pain condition (fibromyalgia).

- Hadley (she/her) is half Latina and lesbian.

Content Warnings

- Some language

- Some sexual content (mild, fade-to-black)

- Minor injury with blood

Dedication

For anyone who has known the brilliant pain and beauty of loving
someone the way Amelia and Hadley love each other.

CHAPTER ONE

Her best friend smelled like jasmine petals in a rainstorm and for Amelia, that scent meant home. Her free-spirited, world traveling, easy come, easy go best friend had used the same perfume oil for years. Every time she picked Hadley up from the airport or the train station, they hugged. Cried a little. And Amelia would bury her face in her friend's dark, wavy hair and seek out that scent. Hadley knew she wasn't the touchy-feely type and never once denied Amelia her gentle touch, but this hug, the one that said *Hi, I missed you, I'm so glad to see you*, was always the tightest. The one where Amelia remembered what jasmine smelled like once again.

The wave of nostalgia and caramel-sugar sweetness that hit Amelia as she watched Hadley poke through cartons of wine took the air from her lungs as readily as that scent did. Hadley was staring straight down at her clipboard, pen in her left hand while her right hovered over the bottles in the nearest crate. That thick hair was pulled back from her heart-shaped face by a bandana, and her willowy frame was nearly lost in baggy plum overalls. But Hadley, ever the rebel, didn't let sharp crate edges or itchy packing material bother her; not when there was a crop top to wear. It wasn't like wearing a suit to a sack race, but Amelia had to smile at her dearest friend's insistence on wearing something that gave the big middle finger to the task at hand. In true Hadley fashion, she was daring the crates and packing material to come at her, and if they did, she'd kick them out of the way with her steel-toed boots.

Hadley turned, found Amelia in the doorway, and said, "Are all of these wines so pretentious sounding?" She pulled a face. "Ah yes, the thirty-year old *pinot grigio* grown in a hydroponic garden located in an abandoned silo -"

Amelia had to laugh. "That would never happen. Grapes need proper sun and soil. Hydroponics won't cut it." She took the wine bottle from Hadley and turned it over to inspect the label. "This is a fifteen-dollar bottle and it's from California." Amelia walked over and picked up the bottle at the top-right of the crate. "Nine times out of ten, if the label is trying to look old or rich, or the name is some weird bastardization of French or Spanish, it's a table wine meant to make people feel fancy. Nothing wrong with that, but I won't upsell products or promise something outside of what customers can see and taste." She set the bottle back down and peered over at Hadley's clipboard. "Yeah, I bought duplicates of this crate. It's one of the best-selling wines I could get my hands on for the opening."

Hadley smirked. She had a mole by the edge of one sweetly bowed lip and Amelia let her gaze slip away from it. And Hadley's mouth. "So the best seller is the...gas station beer of wine?"

"Maybe a salted rim margarita. Predictable but pretty tasty if you're looking for a few drinks."

"Can we open one?"

"It's ten am, Hads."

Hadley waggled her eyebrows. "When has that ever stopped me?"

Amelia could never resist her. Could almost never say no.

They drank that one bottle over the course of the day and Amelia got to see how the sun, or lack thereof, changed the interior of the store. Watching washed-out sunlight splash across the brick walls and gray stone floors made something in her chest pop open in relieved happiness. Finally, she could see the light at the end of the tunnel; her dream realized. None of the struggles up to this point mattered in those moments where she could picture the space not full of haphazard crates and trash bags and the scent of paint lingering in her nostrils; but one full of life and enjoyment, a spot welcoming to everyone. Classy Corks didn't mean snobbish adherence to old (white) standards and ridiculous beliefs about "wine culture". It didn't cater to "wine moms"' or urban socialites, nor would it clearance-bin itself to selling wine that tasted like aspartame and lost dreams.

Welcoming to everyone meant *everyone* and what Amelia wanted to cultivate was a warm space where wine and comfort and laughter went hand in hand. She had immediately liked the calm vibe of Breakwater, but after being in town for a few weeks, she'd realized it was as close to her kind of perfect she'd ever find. And she'd signed the lease that day, knowing the next several months would be full of hard work. The kind of hard work that was worth it.

And now Hadley was here and everything was brighter. Better.

"Ames?"

Amelia looked up at her friend — her brilliant, sunny, nothing-can-take-me-down Hadley — and smiled. She knew exhaustion pulled at the corners of her mouth but she didn't have to hide the fatigue. For one, Hadley would kill her, and two, she understood. "I think this is the last of the middle shelf stock," she said, motioning to the two open crates to her right. "If we can get this set on the shelves, we're ahead of schedule."

That got her a grin, gap toothed and so earnest Amelia felt like she'd been punched in the heart. Hadley crossed the space between them and wrapped her arms around Amelia's middle, resting her chin on Amelia's shoulder. It made her body ache a little bit more, but she'd never *ever* say anything. The thought of Hadley moving away from the embrace was like a cold prickle over her skin. She would never. "You are amazing," Hadley said softly, stirring a bit of red hair that had fallen out of Amelia's bun. "I don't know another soul who could do what you've already accomplished with this place."

She snorted, but the compliment hit. Right on target. Another punch to the heart. All she could do was tighten her arms around Hadley. "You're full of shit."

"I'm not and you know it."

Another sigh but she let it take her back, until she and Hadley were pressed against each other and all she could smell was jasmine. "I know."

"So, let me finish those crates. Don't you have paperwork or something boring to do?"

"And leave you with all the heavy lifting?"

"Ames."

"What?"

"It's two crates."

She knew there was no use arguing. But her stubborn ass was going anyway. "Yeah. One for me, one for you."

"Nope." Hadley popped the *p*. "All mine. I'm a greedy jerk like that."

No, I think I am, she wanted to say because Hadley was then running her hands up Amelia's arms, thumbs pressing just right into her muscles. She groaned and hung her head. "Should let me look after you, now that I'm here."

"Hadley -"

"I know, I know. Stubborn to a fault." More delicious pressure into her exhausted, aching muscles as Hadley's touch slid higher, and then she was rubbing circles into Amelia's shoulders. She wanted to fall to the floor and let Hadley do whatever she wanted. She wanted to be a puddle of goo, without a thought in her head. Amelia knew her body would be screaming at her in the morning if she was lucky. The pain might start tonight and then she wouldn't be able to make dinner and enjoy their evening on the porch.

Their evening. The thing she'd been looking forward to all day, warm comfort food over glasses of wine, and then later, cups of tea. Sitting together on the old rocker in the garden, watching twilight descend on that tiny place where nothing mattered but the two of them.

"Hold on." Amelia wiggled out of Hadley's grip, making her friend protest, but she waved her off. "Hold on." Her bag was near the back door, and as she bent to dig through the front pocket, something in her back *screamed*. Even though she was used to pain on a certain level, this was the kind of thing that made her vision white out. Amelia bit back a gasp as her fingers curled around the key ring. She stood, keeping her face neutral, and came back to Hadley, hand outstretched. "You're staying with me."

Hadley stared hard at the key she held up. She could almost hear the gears clicking in her friend's mind. Hadley would have stayed somewhere outside town, thinking Amelia would, in her typical fashion, want and need her space. But in truth, she wanted nothing more than Hadley to stay with her, tucked away in the little cottage she was renting. It wasn't Hadley's kind of space; probably too quaint and lacking quirky furniture or backwards faucet handles. But it did look like the inside of a witch's cabin and *that* would appeal to her best friend's more hippy, smell-the-roses-and-hug-the-trees side. She cast a glance up at the brick walls and smiled, knowing Hadley would help her fill the space with those unique pieces people would look at and discuss over wine and remember the next time they came in.

Next time

Because Breakwater was now home, and the mere thought of such a thing left her weak-kneed and shaky. Home. In a cute little place like this, with its square and its market and adorable pet population and all the people she'd yet to meet, the friends she'd yet to make.

Having Hadley here was a wonderful start. Because this was home.

"You're staying with me," Amelia finally said as she pressed the key into Hadley's palm. "No arguments."

"N-no. No arguments." Her friend's eyes were huge and hopeful. "But -"

"No arguments."

Hadley's answer was to launch herself into Amelia's arms and laugh into her hair and leave Amelia feeling foolish and loved all at the same time.

CHAPTER TWO

When Amelia said *cottage*, Hadley immediately smelled pine and citrus, saw polished but worn wood floors, cozy nooks, and heavy, handmade quilts. Pin-neat, a little old-fashioned. Exactly the kind of place Amelia would like.

She sure as hell hadn't expected what looked like the inside of a witch's brothel. So she said as much. "Ames. What the fuck."

Amelia lingered on the threshold, keys clenched in her hand as she leaned heavily against the doorframe. "Shit. I thought you'd like it."

"I fucking *love it*. Holy hells." Hadley whirled, grinning, arms outstretched as if to take in the whole place. Like she could feel its essence slipping through her. The drapey fabrics and fraying embroidery, the crooked drawers and squeaky doors, the herbs and plants and tassels and thick, velvety cushions. The very air felt right and while it was a weird thought, Hadley leaned into it.

But Amelia was looking at her with expectation and it all clicked. Fucking hell. "Did you rent this place for us?"

"It's better than a hotel. It's close to town but far enough out to see the stars." One corner of Amelia's mouth tugged up into a smile. "And I figured there's enough here for both of us to like. If you want to stay, that is."

Hadley wanted to squeeze her. Squeeze her and never let her go and take care of her *always always always*. Because for so long, Ames had taken care of her. Hadley's payment was long overdue. She'd never ever say anything like that to Ames's face, of course, unless she wanted a stern tongue-lashing.

Do. Not. Think. Like. That.

Because thoughts of tongues and Amelia quickly got bound up in her most secret fantasy, the one that still colored her face with shame even as she let it play about her mind in the humid dark while she gasped. It was rotten, that thing; some curse, befouling and besieging.

A terrible thing to be in love with your best friend.

And for Hadley, she'd been from the start. Head over heels in what she thought was love at eight years old and watching Ames's bright red ponytail bounce as they hopped across chalk squares. Hadley could remember the scent of sunshine on hot pavement and the way pollen from the garden floated on the wind. It had been mid-July and humid as anything, and Amelia's family had just moved in next door. They were instantly friends and Hadley had been so happy to see another girl her age. Growing up in a house full of boys would do that, and even though she was the youngest, Hadley had never liked being anyone's "princess." She scabbed her knees and ran through the woods and jumped in the mud like the rest of them.

Amelia didn't do those things, not wanting to get dirty. And that didn't matter. Because Amelia was smart and liked books and bugs, and they'd take their library books to the garden behind Amelia's house and read until Hadley's dad leaned over the fence and told her it was time for dinner.

She had buckets of those memories, so happy and full of joy. Buckets of days, of experiences; gray ones where rain lashed at the windows but she and Ames were safe and warm and dry inside her room, giggling and poking each other, or the sun-drenched ones where they ran and chased, kicking soccer balls back and forth, occasionally tumbling to the ground. If she concentrated, she could remember so many days where Amelia was there. More than a presence, but a fixture, a known quantity, in her life.

Her best friend. Her first love. Her *only* love.

Hadley had long ago realized that the way she loved Amelia was like no other feeling in the world. It wasn't blind obsession or a childhood crush.

They were friends.

But *friends* didn't cover the depth of her love for Amelia. It couldn't.

Amelia was the most important person in her life. And like the good cliché went, Hadley had long ago realized her love was unrequited. Oh, she'd never *asked*, of course. Why the hell would she do that? But Amelia was the kind of person who, once an idea was in her head and the plan was laid out, could not be deterred from her path. She was as stubborn as anyone Hadley had ever met, and Hadley been around the world several times by this point. If she loved Hadley like that, she would have said so.

So Hadley put that love on a shelf, kept it safe, took it down to look at it on occasion. Sometimes it sat there for months, or even years, as she worked and traveled, had flings and occasionally fell for a woman in Greece or Brazil. But then, eventually, the quiet dark would set in and she'd take that little box down and look at that bit of her heart no one could ever touch except Ames and she'd weep.

And yet, there was no fault ascribed to anyone but herself. Because she'd been the one to fall in love, and fall *hard*. So hard that no one else could ever match up to red hair and wide, expressive eyebrows, and a soft voice that could go stern in an instant. Ames liked denim and flannel and linen, and today she'd been in old, worn jeans, heavy boots, and a blue flannel open to her navel and tied in a knot; the thin undershirt growing damp as they worked. Hadley certainly hadn't snuck a glance or two. Amelia was hard to ignore.

Amelia was now leaning into her, an arm over Hadley's shoulders, strong fingers gripping tight. She was warm and somehow still smelled like sawdust and sunshine after a hard day's work. "You okay?"

"I just...of course I want to stay. Are you kidding?" Hadley spun and grabbed Amelia tight. "It's *gorgeous!*" She darted into the little reading nook in the front of the cottage, no more than a windowed corner with a rickety bookshelf filled with battered paperbacks, dried flowers, glinting little crystals, and other weird bric-a-brac. The armchair, however...oh, what an armchair. It was really big enough to be two armchairs. The fabric was plush velvet; a little worn-white on the corners and Hadley could see scratched wooden legs. But she and Amelia would fit very nicely in that chair. Together.

Hadley shook that last thought away. It wasn't anything she could have. Sure, she could teasingly sit beside Amelia in the chair and poke and pester her until she gave up with whatever smutty romance book she was reading and paid attention. But Amelia would only take it as friendly teasing. And that would hurt more than the promise of getting to tangle her fingers in Amelia's curls and bare a pale, freckled throat. Amelia's gasps would fill her ears and send her stomach swooping with pleasure. In that fantasy, Hadley didn't poke or prod; she teased with intention and longing. She drew out gentle moans and soft gasps and left Amelia sated and exhausted.

"The owner said we can read anything, and likes to have people take from and add to the collection." Amelia plucked out a biography on Joan of Arc. Dust and the scent of old paper filled the small space between them. "And if you leave a book, sign it with your initials and the month and year." She flipped to the front and saw a "T.E., May 1993" scribbled there. "I bet all these books have been touched by some other guest. All those people looking for stories." She sighed happily and Hadley grinned.

"I never want to hear you say you're not a romantic," Hadley whispered. Her fingers itched to take hold of Amelia's waist, to pluck the tucked-in flannel away so she could feel warm skin. But if she took that chance and lied one more time that it was friendly, loving, *chaste*...she'd never forgive herself. "You know why books smell like that?"

"I don't." Amelia was tracing her fingers over the cover, following along the yellowed creases and cracks.

"I was in Cambridge a few years back and working in an old bookshop. A professor came in, very proper English and all that. Except for his fabulous hair, long and white and braided to the middle of his back. And he and I started talking and he'd come in once a week and we'd talk about poetry. And when I mentioned that scent being full of memories, he said it was because books were memories of trees and what they could have been, if they'd been allowed to touch the sky."

Amelia's next breath was a sigh dipped in melancholy. "That was maybe the most beautiful and depressing thing I've ever heard." And then she snorted and Hadley laughed and the air between them balanced out once more. Amelia balanced her out. Her best friend, and her only love.

The evening passed in a dreamy kind of way Amelia loved. Her back wasn't hurting so much that she couldn't take up half the dinner prep. But in the middle of the last carrot for their stir fry, her hand cramped and the knife went to the floor, narrowly missing her slipper.

"Shit."

Hadley was there immediately. "You okay?" she asked as she came over, spatula in hand, a piece of onion clinging to the square, metal scoop.

"I'm good, I just need to..." She started to bend forward to pick up the knife, but her hand cramped again. The pain was so sudden, so hot, that it took her to the floor. Great. She'd probably have a bruise on her ass tomorrow. No matter how careful she was, it couldn't be easier to earn badges of mottled green and purple while doing the most mundane tasks.

"I got it." Hadley swooped in and picked up the knife, then set it and the spatula aside to cast her grip down to Amelia. "You are going to sit and have a glass of wine while I finish dinner."

"Hads -" She was truly glad for the help. Amelia hated asking, and Hadley knew it. She never begrudged the help from Hadley, but some days it threatened to burn. She was stressed with the winery and probably a little thin-skinned of late. That was all.

"Up you go." Hadley hauled her to her feet and grinned. "Go. Sit. Down. I got this." And she did. Amelia had a glass of malbec in her hand a moment later while Hadley cooked and bopped around to the little portable speaker she'd pulled out of her bags before they'd gotten started.

Amelia didn't want to linger on how lopsided Hadley's apron bow was, nor the way she moved, hair bouncing, earrings jangling. It wouldn't do her any good. The scratch at the back door was her ticket out. "Oh! Mr. Buttons!"

"What the..."

But Amelia was too focused on opening the back door for a massive, fluffy Maine Coon with dark brown stripes and big green eyes. Tail high, big paws marching, the cat practically jumped into the kitchen and immediately twined around her legs while she laughed. "Mr. Buttons, this is Hadley." She looked up and saw Hadley staring at her with an open mouth and wide eyes. "He's the neighbor's cat but apparently likes it quite a bit over here, too. Made himself at home the first day I was here. The owner's good with it." She held out her arms and Mr. Buttons flew up, landing safely to butt his head against her chin. "I might be spoiling him a little."

Hadley looked *delighted*. Amelia had figured as much. "There is nothing little about that cat. He's all fluff!"

"He's super heavy. He must be like twenty pounds. Trust me, it isn't all fluff." Mr. Buttons *purr-rowed* his assent and rubbed against her one more time before jumping down to pad silently over to Hadley. Hadley, being the kind of person who gladly pet every dog, cat, bird, lizard, snake, ferret, and anything else, immediately crouched to let Mr. Buttons sniff her hand. The purring started back up again and they both laughed.

"He needs a vest," Hadley said once their plates and glasses were full and Mr. Buttons was asleep on a blanket over the scallop-edged sofa. "Do you think that would be okay?"

"I'm sure it is, but he does get into the roses sometimes." Amelia wrinkled her nose. "So maybe nothing too wild."

"I have the best fabric in my bag! I'll show you after dinner." Her friend grinned. "And I have something for you. I hope you like it."

The warm fuzziness that came bundled up in Hadley - her voice, her personality, her gentle hands and jasmine-scented hair - made Amelia's heart ache. It was also near bursting with joy, but with it came a particular kind of pain. Something she couldn't will away; a longing buried deep, written in the very marrow of her bones.

Maybe she should be brave. Take a chance. But not now, not weeks out from a big banner over the door and hopefully a constant stream of new customers from around Breakwater. She couldn't risk it all at once, to have to do it again and lose something. She'd lost enough, and she wasn't ready to break her own heart.

"I'll love it. Always. You know that."

"I know! I just..." Hadley looked away and a curious expression danced across her features.

"Hey." Amelia put her left hand over Hadley's right. "You know that."

"I do. Of course."

Something in Hadley's expression made her sad, made her heart clench. "You okay? Tired from the flight?"

"I am but I want to sit outside. After dinner." Eyes she could never look away from traveled over her face, Hadley's gaze quietly intense. "Come with me? We'll bring out blankets and I have one of those neat hand warmers you can use." Hadley dug in her overall pockets and pulled out a charging cable. "USB and everything and it gets super warm."

"Hads, I'll be all right. The night's aren't too cold anymore."

"Yeah, but the knife."

Ah, that was it. The sharp, shining edge of danger that, had her slippers not possessed a hard shell, could have ended in stitches. Hadley knew Amelia's daily life was pretty mundane, but that had been earned through years of trial and error, stress and pain. She'd been diagnosed with fibromyalgia in college and though she'd kept up with her classes and labs, she'd definitely slipped into doing just enough work to pass. The sourceless pain, the confusion, the memory issues, all of it new and scary and immediately written off by white coats blaming her monthly cycle or *stress*. Amelia had nearly given up at several points along the way, bouncing from appointment to appointment, filling prescriptions for drugs that left her worse off than before. It had been a terrible handful of years, and all she' been left with was a medical term and a load of debt.

She'd grown more tired, more achy, and living on her own came with challenges. Hadley had moved in with her, helped her adapt her living setup for the days that were harder, and generally took care of her. Hadley had seen up-close how bad some days were, and how inexplicable it was that Amelia could be fine a day or two later. They were bound tighter by those weeks and months where Hadley was her second set of hands and eyes. And she'd bought Amelia her first pair of hard-shelled slippers. A silent, sweet gesture of understanding and worry.

Dropping a knife wasn't dropping a towel. Amelia understood that. "Tell you what. We should make tea to go out with us, and you bring out the hand warmer. The spare bedroom has a closet full of blankets, big fluffy ones." Hadley's face lit up and if Amelia had been feeling poetic in the moment, she would have compared it to a cloudless, sunny day and the feel of the wind in her hair. Joy, unadulterated and beautiful.

After dinner, they washed up and Hadley got settled in the guest room while Amelia put the kettle on. She was deciding between oolong and honey green when Hadley came up beside her. "Okay so here's that fabric. It's cute! Polka dots for his stripes."

It was cute; a light green fabric dotted with white and peach circles of different sizes. It almost looked like confetti across the seafoam green. "I like it. Do you still have those melamine orange buttons?"

"Oh, perfect, yes! I have a handful still. And since that's settled..." And then out of Hadley's pocket came a small box. "Quick story before you open it. I went to this junk shop that was supposed to have the most strange, funky stuff. Usually those places are a bust, but I was already on my way through Dublin to the airport. So I swung in, and this was the first thing I saw."

Amelia couldn't ignore the heavy *thump thump thump* of her heart, or the way Hadley's gaze turned expectant. Hopeful. A little fearful. Amelia sucked in a deep breath and gently pried off the lid. A neatly folded square of dark blue silk waited for her, and she pulled back a corner to reveal a key. Not any key; a thick thing of slightly tarnished silver, its teeth elaborate and oddly pleasing to the eye. But the top of the key was a maze of scrollwork, each curve and dip precise, gorgeous. The key had a sparkling silver chain threaded through the top.

"It's a story, right? Putting new life into an old thing. Finally setting up your shop in a cute little brick building in a town that hasn't had such a place before." Hadley's gaze went butter-soft, her mouth relaxed. She reached out to thread her fingers through Amelia's. "A place that hasn't had you before. And you are reviving your sommelier career, going back to what you love. Just because it got put away for a bit doesn't mean it's forgotten. New to old, old to new."

Hadley. Hadley. Her poetess, her scribe. Her romantic dreamer who flitted about but always came back home, to her, to their ...

She couldn't finish the thought. Amelia crushed Hadley to her, swallowing her friend's little *oomph, Ames, damn* in a shuddering breath that left her lightheaded. "It's amazing. I love it." It's all she had to say between deep inhales of jasmine. "Thank you."

And of course Hadley got her a chain with no fussy clasp. The necklace easily slipped over her head and she tightened the toggle until the key rested just below her collarbone. "Thank you," she repeated while Hadley stared at her. "This is so beautiful."

"Yeah, you're uh...you're welcome." Hadley's grip on her shoulders slid down until she could rub Amelia's arms. "So if I give you more gifts, I'll get more hugs. This is the lesson I'm taking away right now."

She had to laugh. If she didn't, she might cry and that would not be good. "You can always have hugs. You know that."

"I know." Hadley grinned at her. "Getting you to admit it is half the fun."

"And I still hug you even after you make fun of me."

"I am not making fun, I'm gently poking fun at your natural stoic self."

"I'm not that stoic."

Hadley danced away from her, laughing as Mr. Buttons swanned in front of her to go to the back door. "Not always! But sometimes."

Hadley's laugh carried on the breeze that wafted in when she opened the door, and Amelia shook her head. "Come back here and make yourself useful."

"Hmm..." Hadley poked her head back around the corner. "Okay. You go outside and burrow into as many blankets as you want. I'll bring the tea." She held up a finger. "Don't argue."

Amelia didn't argue. She let Hadley bring her tea and a very happy Mr. Buttons, and then curled up next to her on the cushioned glider bench. Their cups steamed in the early spring night air, and Mr. Buttons prowled the grey, dry garden beds for whatever he could find.

"This is perfect," Hadley said after several minutes of silence.

"It is." Amelia touched the key and smiled. "How long do you think you'll stay?"

"I was thinking about that." Hadley had been leaning into Amelia but now she reached over and took Amelia's right hand in her own. Clever fingers began pressing into the meat of her palm. "It's cute here. Maybe, if you need help past the opening, I can stay longer. Mum's on another 'extended holiday' with the new rich beau, and she keeps sending money. Maybe I can earn my keep for a change."

Wait. Really? Was Hadley really suggesting... "You want to settle down somewhere?"

"Maybe." Gentle fingers worked their way up her wrist to her forearm. A pleasant buzzing traveled down her spine. It was Hadley's touch and it turned Amelia into goo. Hadley always knew, somehow; always knew where her pain was and how to ease it. "If you think you'll need me."

Always. Always. Gods, what a sight you are, with your jasmine-scented hair and your crop tops, and passport so full you've had to buy three more. The beads you bought in Sri Lanka around your neck, and the little sketching pencils you keep in your bag, the ones that leave blue dye on your fingertips. Those fingertips pressing into me now, making me want to float away because I know you'll be my tether.

"Stay here. I've got the space." It was never a question in her mind. Never, ever once.

"Ames..."

Amelia leaned over and put a finger on Hadley's lips. "No arguing." When Hadley shook her head and then playfully snapped teeth at her finger, Amelia turned her face into that hair and said, "I'm glad you're here."

Hadley's arms wound tight around her. "So am I."

CHAPTER THREE

Four weeks to opening

Hadley had trained a lot of new staff in all the jobs she'd had over the years. Despite her ever-present wanderlust, it was hard to travel when you were working for peanuts, so she'd made the effort over time to cultivate what she called her Wanderlist. A list of people who would either hire her, know where to point her to a role, or otherwise have info on the next place she'd be for more than six months. If she was just bouncing from town to town or country to country, she'd do odd jobs. No commitments, quick money. But she'd stayed in beautiful places across Europe and Central America, places she'd wanted to stay for more than a season or two. So she'd found an apartment, a bike or scooter, and solid employment.

Running small teams in seaside shops, art galleries, and community centers had given her a lot of insight into who would sink or swim in a role. Somehow (though not to Hadley's surprise), Amelia had landed some pretty talented people. The curly-haired shift manager who was learning the cash system from Amelia was a quiet one, but Hadley could see a gleam in their eyes. She liked the determination, the intense stare as they peered over Amelia's shoulder.

"Do you want to give it a try?"

The trainee nodded. "Yeah, I learn better when I do things."

"Great." Amelia waved at Hadley. "Hey, Hads, are you free? Can you play customer for me?"

With a grin, Hadley ambled over to the counter, plucking up a random wine bottle as she passed. Hooking two fingers around the neck of the bottle, she held it aloft and smiled at the trainee. "Hi Sara," she said, noting the name and they/them pronouns on the name tag. "I'm ready to check out."

"Great!" As they'd been trained, Sara waited for Hadley to put the bottle down on the counter before reaching for it. *Never take a bottle from someone cashing out,* Amelia had said. *It can be fumbled or dropped. And if they're an asshole, they might drop it on purpose. It's happened before.* Sara carefully picked up the bottle (they'd get more confident with the more bottles they handled), scanned it with a flick of their wrist, then read off the total. When Hadley handed them a twenty, Sara did everything right, from marking the bill with a counterfeit pen to making change and wrapping and bagging the purchase.

But when Hadley winked at Amelia and said, "Okay, I bought this, right? First sale!," Sara laughed while Amelia rolled her eyes. "I definitely bought this," she faux-whispered to Sara. Then she handed Sara the bag. "And now I'm giving it to you. Congrats on a successful training day."

Sara looked a little flummoxed, but then gently took the bag. "Thanks. I'll enjoy it tonight."

"You did good, Sara. And it's almost time for you to leave, so feel free to go claim a locker before you head out." Her friend's smile was small but encouraging. Exhaustion kept it from fully unfurling. Hadley instantly started making a list of things to do when they got home.

And she tried not to let the *when they got home* part of her thoughts rattle around too much. She didn't need to put any extra meaning behind it when just being near Amelia was enough.

It was enough. It had to be.

Brown curls bouncing, Sara waved to them before disappearing into the back hallway, bag swinging from their left hand. "I like them," Hadley said, smiling. "You have a good eye for talent, babe."

Amelia shrugged. "Honestly, they were one of the best applicants and that's saying something. I actually had a really great pool of people apply, so if someone falls through, I'm hoping I can recall some of the folks I turned down. And most of them I only turned down for a lack of schedule flexibility or experience in retail."

As if an invisible hand pushed her down, Amelia leaned heavily on the counter and sighed. Hadley saw her wince, then watched her friend use her right hand to massage her left. Amelia's hands bothered her a lot some days; redness, swelling, pain. She'd described it as a persistent, dull ache that sometimes flared hot or felt like she was being stabbed in the thumb. Hadley knew better than to apologize. Amelia used to brush off those sincere, but ineffective words so instead, Hadley had started to ask what Amelia needed. And now years later, Hadley usually had a game plan in mind.

"Was Sara the last one today?" Hadley asked as she rounded the counter and pulled Amelia in close with a firm arm around her waist. Amelia mumbled something but didn't raise her head from where she was resting it on stacked forearms. "Can you stand up straight?" Another mumble and Hadley snickered softly. "Okay, now you're being stubborn."

Amelia's arm shot up, middle finger in the air.

"Well, if that's how you want to be, then none of my special tea for you."

Very slowly, Amelia turned her head until Hadley could see one hazel eye narrowed. "How dare you."

"I can be just as stubborn as you."

"You're *so* mean."

"I am. Very mean. Grrr."

Laughing, Amelia pushed off the counter, wobbled, and Hadley caught her with both hands. "Thanks."

Amelia was very close. Sappy romance movie close-up *close*. Her best friend staring right into her eyes. Long red hair begging to be touched. Hadley knew how Amelia liked to have her hair played with; knew how to pull the springy curls into a tight French braid. Years of practice during slumber parties had created special muscle memory just for those braids.

And Hadley was weak. If she couldn't grab Amelia by the hips and slot their mouths together in the way she wanted (*the way she wanted to lick inside Amelia's mouth and make her whimper, to taste her the way she deserved*), she could reach out and tangle her fingers in that beautiful hair. Almost brown but with a deep flush of honey-red staining every strand.

Hadley ran her fingertips over Amelia's scalp, from behind her ear and up. Eyes fluttering shut, Amelia said, "Keep doing that and I'll be putty."

"I like putty. It means you're relaxed."

"Hmmm."

"Ames."

"Huh?"

"Ready to go?"

Amelia's soft noise of dissent made her smile. "I promise I will do this again for you tonight."

"Fine." Amelia only sounded put-out. Hadley knew she was only assenting to leaving before nightfall because they had a full day ahead of them tomorrow.

With what looked like regret, Amelia slowly backed away and left to gather her things, leaving Hadley to nab hers from a nearby table. It had been a week since she'd moved into Amelia's little rented cottage and so far, it had been utter bliss. They worked hard during the day, and the shop showed it. In her mind's eye, Hadley could picture the place buzzing: customers browsing shelves and poking through jars of glass stoppers; booking appointments to go into the "Winebrary," where the rare bottles were kept and the wine tastings held; and sitting at the concrete bistro tables with full glasses.

It was going to be brilliant.

"What's that look for?"

Hadley turned and saw Amelia smiling at her, head cocked to the side. "I was just thinking about how great this place is. How welcoming and fucking cool."

"High praise." Amelia held out her arm in invitation, which Hadley of course took. "Praise I more than appreciate, of course."

"Of course." That old ache was back as soon as they touched like this. Like friends forever, casual and sweet but platonic. The ache of wanting what she couldn't have, the ache of knowing it would never be that way. The ache of loving someone so close and so far away. On days like this, it flared hot under her skin and then began a relentless tattoo like a drumbeat.

The selfish, needy part of her wanted Amelia in that way. But the rest of her knew that having anything as close as it was now — living together, working together, making eggs together, drinking wine in the little garden together — was good enough.

"Ready to go home?"

Of course she was. Close was enough. It had to be.

Amelia's phone buzzed just as Hadley handed her a cup of tea. The cottage came fully stocked, from rugs to furniture to mismatched plates and bowls and cups, and it was all delightfully kitsch. The cup in her hand was handmade ceramic, with a hand warmer handle and cute chanterelle mushrooms sprouting in an arc around the left side. She was admiring the mushrooms' gentle curve around the cup when two text messages lit up her screen. The first one was from her mother, asking how the shop was coming along. But the second was a tracking number from a delivery service. She combed through her memory, going through everything for the store that had yet to be shipped out or was on its way. Nothing was coming from overseas, and certainly nothing in a large, square box.

It was probably a spam message. Amelia sipped her blackberry tea - Hadley's special blend that she could never get enough of - and let her thumb hover over the link. Something twitched in the back of her mind; an instinct. Maybe it *was* something that had been rerouted?

"You okay?"

"Huh?" Amelia looked up as Hadley settled next to her on the glider and pulled the big, hand-knitted blanket over her lap. Snuggled together like this as night settled around them and their tea cups steamed into the air, Amelia was able to sigh and relax. "Oh, it's this message." She turned her phone so Hadley could see. But her always opinionated friend was strangely quiet as she barely glanced at the screen. "It's probably spam. I'll just delete it."

"No, don't!" Panic wrote itself across Hadley's face and Amelia immediately frowned, worried. "It's uh...shit. It wasn't supposed to arrive this fast! Not that I'm going to grouse about it showing up early, but I told the artist to take her time."

"Okay. So, you know what this is?"

Hadley took a sip of her tea then pulled a face. "Fuck. Okay, that's too hot. Shit, Ames, I'm so sorry. I wanted it to show up right before opening."

Oh, Hadley. Sweet, caring, *throw it all to the wind because fuck it, you only have one life* Hadley.

"Can you just...hit the link for me?" Hadley was batting her eyelashes but Amelia knew she was worried. She did this little thing with her brow when anxiety clouded her mind. "Please."

"Yeah. Yeah, of course. But Hads, what did you do?"

Both shoulders rose up and Hadley gave a soft chuckle. "What I always do."

She didn't have to say any more. Amelia opened the tracking link and the next screen popped up, showing a rather large box coming from France; it was currently sitting on a container ship and would be at the next destination in a few days.

"It's a gift for you. For the shop, if you want. I found an artist while I was in France and she makes the most beautiful things."

Her hand immediately went to the key around her neck. "Hads, you can't....you already got me something."

"Yeah, well....I mean, this is custom made and it should fit the shop! But if it doesn't, that's okay and maybe you can find somewhere else to put it. Or, I can always send it back." Hadley's tone grew softer and Amelia could see doubt creep in, a thief in the shadows ready to steal her friend's joy.

Amelia's heart melted. "Don't you dare. Whatever it is, it'll be perfect." She gripped Hadley's hand harder. "Don't you dare. You always think of me and that's..."

How could she say what lived in her heart, what flowered there and made her feel so light, so wonderful? How could she even begin to try and put words to the emotions that rattled through her? Everything about Hadley had always been special, and pressed to give an answer to when she'd fallen in love with her best friend, Amelia wouldn't be able to.

Maybe she'd always been a little bit in love with Hadley. Maybe those nights pining over someone she couldn't have weren't wasted, but were instead new growth, new maturity. She was no moody, starry-eyed teenager nor a twenty-something trying to find footing in a world stacked against her. Love had never been something that came easily to her. Hell, she'd been accused by more than one ex of being "withdrawn" or "distant". Though "cold" was the only word that had ever been more than a papercut. "Cold" had hurt in a way she never could explain, even to this day. That same ex had remarked how much more alive Amelia seemed when Hadley was around.

Her head spun as she held tight to Hadley's hand and stared into that heart-shaped face. "Don't you dare," she whispered. "Everything you do for me is special."

You are special, her heart sang, but she couldn't force the words up and into the air.

Then Hadley, in her sweet, soft way that made Amelia's teeth itch and her hands ache in a different kind of sense, smiled and held her arms out. "Okay. Okay. Whew. Come here, please. I need a hug really badly."

Amelia curled up in Hadley's arms and pressed her cheek into the soft, worn fabric of her hoodie. She felt Hadley relax, felt the clench of long-fingered hands at her waist and shoulder. Felt her sigh and how it stirred her hair. But the breath Hadley took before speaking was what reverberated through her. Like standing at a precipice and wondering what lay beyond.

"Do you know how special you are, Ames?"

Amelia frowned. "What?"

Very gently — so gently, it was as if the wind itself helped to move her — Hadley turned her until they were face to face, Amelia practically splayed out in her friend's lap. It was a *difficult* position to be in, though not wholly foreign to them. Often Hadley would pull Amelia back against her to braid her hair or rub her sore shoulders.

But this felt different. Good, but different. There was that precipice looming large, but the horizon beyond so, so promising.

"I don't know what I'd do without you." Hadley's confession was a whisper nearly lost on the breeze. "Every time I'm with you, I'm home. I want to be home all the time any more. I want...." Hadley turned away, face pinched. "I love traveling, but I've been to a lot of places. I thought home was wherever I was happiest but I kept thinking that was the next place." She reached up to tangle her fingers in Amelia's hair. "I need you. Home is you."

Every response flew out of her mind, a flock of birds leaving behind their nests for the winter. She gave in to the desire thrumming through her and tucked her face into Hadley's neck, smelling jasmine and blackberry and holding back the hot tears that wanted to spill. "Don't you dare go anywhere," she mumbled. "Don't you dare."

"But if you ever want me out of your hair -"

Amelia lifted her head and gave Hadley her best death stare. "No."

Despite the shake in her voice, Hadley laughed softly. "Okay, okay."

"I mean it, Hads."

Gods, please stay with me. Don't leave again.

"But you have to let me buy more groceries and cook better stuff."

Amelia nodded. She wasn't a very good cook outside of the basics, but Hadley could whip up beautiful, savory meals in a heartbeat. Like a culinary magic trick. "I won't say no."

"I didn't think you would." Hadley patted her own shoulder. "Now come back. Please."

Amelia slowly relaxed against Hadley and listened to the steady beat of the heart beneath her ear while she lost track of where the wind and Hadley's soft breaths stirred her hair.

When she woke up, Hadley was quietly humming while she rubbed Amelia's left hand with her right. "Should probably get you inside, babe."

"Yeah." Her body *ached* and she'd hurt tomorrow, too, but she didn't regret the time spent curled up against Hadley. As if that were her natural habitat, the only space she could live and fully let go. Hadley got them both to their feet and then steered Amelia inside, shutting off lights and checking doors as they went. The bedrooms were on the cottage's second floor, more of an extended loft than a true upper story. The rooms were identical in layout and across the short hall from each other. Amelia managed to stumble into her doorway and turn, only to find Hadley carefully watching her every move.

"I'm okay," she grouched.

Hadley just shook her head and smiled. "I know you are. But I want to make sure you get your rest. If you're up for it, I would love to visit some spots in town in the morning."

Downtown Breakwater was about as cute as it could get, but Amelia had yet to visit any of the shops. Classy Corks had needed too much attention and by the time she left in the evenings, most places were long shut down. "You should definitely go."

"Yes, and you're coming with me."

Amelia had figured Hadley would say that. Part of her wanted to argue; there was still so much to do. But she also knew she needed the break, and running herself ragged to the breaking point would be detrimental to actual progress on the store. So she nodded and instead said, "All right. But only in the morning. And then in the afternoon, I'll have some of the decorations you helped me pick out arriving. We can hang those up."

For a moment, Hadley's nose scrunched like it did when she wanted to argue. "You've learned the art of compromise? My Amelia?" She put a hand to her chest. "I never thought I'd see the day."

"Okay, if you're just going to make fun of me, I'm going to bed."

"Noooo, don't do that! Anything but that!"

Laughing, Amelia stepped further into her room. "I love you, but you're ridiculous."

"I know, I know. Oh, wait, come here!" Hadley crossed the hallway in two steps and then was tugging Amelia into a hug. "I'm so proud of you," she said into Amelia's hair. "So proud of you."

She would not cry. She wouldn't. Amelia managed to keep her reaction to a sniffle before pulling back slightly. "Thank you. I...that means a lot."

Hadley brushed her hair back, her touch gentle once more. "You work so hard, babe. I'm going to make sure you take care of yourself."

"Or you'll do it for me?"

"Don't you threaten me with a good time, Amelia de Ville."

Then Hadley kissed her forehead and stepped back, taking her warmth and her scent with her. It made Amelia want to beg her to *come back, stay, please, don't leave me alone.*

But of course she said none of that. She waved good night, shut her door, and then slumped against it, as if the old wood could take more than just her weight but her emotions, too.

Sweet Tarts Bakery was possibly the cutest thing Amelia had ever seen, and she wasn't normally a big fan of *cute*. Though, to be fair, *cute* could be the word to describe the entire town, through a certain point of view. The window boxes shaking off winter, the narrow streets over which balconies hung, and the shop signs creaking in the early spring breeze. And then the buildings, a mix of mid-century brick and older, more rambling architecture with brightly painted doorways and restored woodwork and the occasional flashing neon sign. In the distance, scaffolding on other buildings stood tall and proud, and Amelia saw figures moving about on the roofs. She elbowed Hadley, who looked over. "Already working, even in the cold," Hadley said. "Man, they take their town seriously. But that's a good thing."

"Yeah, I think I got really lucky. The building the shop's in had very little that needed fixed, which is surprising given the age of the town."

Hadley hooked her arm into Amelia's. "That just means you were supposed to be here."

"Yeah. Yeah, I think so."

The town was still waking up as they strolled down Main Street but they weren't the only ones lured in by the scents of coffee and sugar; a steady stream of customers kept the door from closing all the way as they approached. A dark haired woman in her twenties seated at an outdoor table had on a leash the biggest poodle possibly in existence, all black fluff and huge brown eyes. The dog swiveled its head as they approached and the young woman smiled. Amelia had seen her and the dog around but hadn't yet taken the time to greet them.

"Can we say hello?" Amelia asked. With Hadley practically vibrating with excitement at her side, she figured now would be a good time to make introductions.

The woman waved them over. "New in town?"

"Yes! Sorry, I mean *yes*." Hadley approached slowly, hand out, and soon had a massive snout sniffing her palm. "Oh. Oh. I love him. Immediately. This dog is my soulmate."

"Hey." But Amelia only sounded affronted to get another one of Hadley's smiles. "Fine, toss me aside for a dog."

"This is not any dog, this is a gentle giant," Hadley crooned as she stooped to rub the dog's ears. "Best day of this last...month, except for when I got my hug."

"Oh, that's so sweet." The woman was looking at them with a soft expression. "You two are adorable."

And for once, Amelia didn't have a response. With everything swirling in her mind and upending her emotions, what could she say? That she was right and then confess her love to Hadley in front of half the town?

Sure, maybe if it was a cheesy romance movie. But this was real and there were decades of tangled emotions involved and she had a shop to open and...and...

"Does he wear clothes? Because I would *love* to knit him a sweater." Hadley was totally focused on the dog, unaware of Amelia's plight. Which was for the better.

"He does!" the woman exclaimed. "He doesn't need them, and doesn't always want them on. Especially on days like today, where the sun's out and it's a little warmer. But I'll gladly pay you for something."

"Oh no, not at all. This is my gift to you and your beautiful dog that I *love so much and I just want to rub his ears all day*." The sheer delight in Hadley's voice drew Amelia's gaze back to them, and when she looked, she realized their little conversation was drawing a few onlookers posted up in the short line forming to get inside the baker.

Hadley was drawing a crowd. Not shocking at all. She was always good at that, commanding the attention of a room with her sweetheart face and bright eyes and long, wavy hair. Hair that today was half up in a knot on the top of her head and sparkling from a little beaded chain she'd wrapped around it. Her thick red sweater and grey leggings were not without trademark touches, from the tasseled, multi-colored scarf down her back and the goldenrod socks peeking out above grey boots; all of it made Hadley look like the glittering, bubbly sprite Amelia knew her to be.

It made her heart thunder to look at Hadley having such a great time while others looked on. The selfish part of her wanted to keep Hadley for herself, all that color and energy shimmering around her; but that was part of what she loved most about her best friend. How, no matter where she went, people wanted to talk to her, to interact with her, to laugh and smile and feel as though they were the center of that happy little world.

I love you

The words were right there. She could say them now and watch ruination take hold, sweeping away everything good. Or she could, as usual, hold it in, tend to it like a gardener, and watch it flourish. There was still time to confess, after all. There would always be time.

CHAPTER FOUR

Three weeks to opening

"Is she okay?"

Hadley turned to give Sara the next bottle to stack on the shelves and replied, "Who?"

"Amelia." Sara frowned and it marred their narrow, almost feline features. "She's been in the back for a while."

"In her office?" Hadley's mind flashed with a warning signal, but she shook it off.

Amelia was probably fine.

"No, in the stock room. She asked me to come out here and help with the shelves, but she said she'd be right out." Dark brows drew down in confusion. "I'll go check on her."

"No, you stay and keep shelving, you're doing great. I'll get her." Hadley smiled, trying not to sound or look concerned. "She probably got stuck in an inventory spreadsheet, knowing her."

"Okay." But Sara was still frowning. Hadley gave them a pat to the shoulder before taking off at a jog to the back of the store. She passed the bathrooms and offices to the keycard door that led to the stock room and loading dock. "Hey, Ames?"

Silence.

Shit.

"Ames? You okay?"

Finally, a thin voice replied. "Hadley, can you come back here?"

And now she was very worried. Hands cold, Hadley swiped her card once and when the display let red, she swore and tried it again. And again. On the third pass, with frustration mounting so much she was ready to rip the door from its hinges, the scanner finally beeped and lit up green. And then she was racing inside, looking left to right until, over the top of a crate, she spotted a wild mass of red curls up in a bandana. "Ames!"

"I'm okay." But Amelia didn't sound okay. Her voice was tight and low, threaded through with pain. And when Hadley rounded the crate, she didn't look okay either. Amelia's face was bone-white but there was sweat on her brow and a few curls of red hair clung there. Hadley was immediately at her side, kneeling in the dust so she could take stock of the situation and help Amelia. The stepstool they used for the higher inventory shelves was on its side, one of its plastic legs cracked. Amelia's phone was at least twenty feet away and out of easy reach. The screen was spiderwebbed with a large crack, the kind that would make using the thing near impossible.

And there was blood on the floor.

Just a few bright red drops, but any blood was too much. Amelia was cradling her left hand, but her face spoke of more pain than a cut. "Okay, what do you need? We have bandages in the bathroom."

"Cut myself on the tape dispenser. But I fell off the stepstool trying to grab it, and I'm having trouble getting back up."

Not good. Amelia was tough, and not just in a "I'm good with pain" kind of way. Her dearest friend was often stubborn to a fault, and it would take something like this to make her frightened. One of Amelia's biggest fears was falling, and she studiously avoided anything that looked slippery or cracked; she was as likely to dodge a wet spot on the floor as she avoided uneven sidewalk stones. Time and time again,

Hadley had watched her detour into the grass or hop to another part of the floor to reduce the chance of tripping or falling.

I can't fall. I'll hit hard and it'll be just pain for days. I can't add that to how I feel every day.

She'd never forgotten that confession after Amelia had turned down an invite to go ice skating years ago. It had been a long, trying endeavor for Amelia to get some kind of diagnosis, but no matter the quality or quantity of physical therapy sessions or medications, falling was still a massive fear.

Heart in her throat, Hadley asked, "What do you need me to do?"

All Amelia could manage was a weak, "Please help me up."

She'd do more than that. She'd take Amelia home and bundle her up and find heating pads and ice packs and make tea. Anything at all to soothe the ache. Even if she couldn't cure it, she'd get Amelia whatever she wanted and needed.

Under Amelia's direction, Hadley stooped to let her reach up and wrap lanky arms around her neck. Thankfully, Amelia's legs were uninjured and her hand was only cut a little, so Hadley could devote all her attention to ensuring her friend's back and sides weren't jostled. Slowly, with Amelia death-gripping her and apologizing in the same breath, Hadley got them to their feet.

But the pain on Amelia's face told a story her silence hid.

"I'm taking you home."

As she expected, Amelia fought back. "I just need -"

"A hot bath and some tea and as much muscle balm as we can slather you in. No arguing."

"The store. Hadley." Those big, brown eyes hit her with a wave of sadness that nearly knocked Hadley's feet out from under her. "I can't leave it. There's too much to do."

"It'll be there in the morning. We'll stay late tomorrow, and over the weekend." Hadley gestured at the stockroom. "Look at this. Look what you've built, Ames. It's *incredible*." As she pressed her cheek into Amelia's temple, she whispered, "You're incredible And it's time you understood just how much."

Upon opening the door to the cottage, Hadley immediately went into caretaker mode. The drive over had been silent other than to ask Amelia if she was all right (and not do it a million times, so she kept it just a few). And now Amelia was cursing under her breath and staggering inside.

"Tell me where."

"It just hurts. I'll be all right."

Hadley wanted to growl or curse. Amelia's stubbornness wasn't unearned when it came to her pain. It was her body and she'd been the one living with her condition for many years. But being stubborn was one thing; it was another to not let your best friend take care of you. And it was a battle Amelia wasn't going to win this time. Hadley had conceded so much ground over the years. Not this time, not now.

"You are going to sit somewhere you're as comfortable as possible."

"Hadley -"

"Amelia." With a deep breath, Hadley stopped in front of Amelia, hands on her shoulders, and said, "Please. I'm going to make you tea or whatever you want. And while you're drinking that, I'm going to fill up the tub." She pressed her thumbs into bunched muscles between Amelia's neck and shoulders and got the exact reaction she was hoping for. A soft groan and Amelia letting her head fall forward to rest against Hadley's collarbone. She dropped her voice into a whisper, hoping Amelia would hear her. *Really* hear her. Really hear the love and adoration she held for the one person in the world who made her feel *incredible*. Not just important or loved — those were needed, yes — but truly *incandescent*. Every time Hadley was with Amelia, that's how she felt. And she'd never been able to give voice to it until now. "Let me take care of you. Anything you want, tell me."

The long silence that followed left Hadley counting their breaths. In and out, in and out; soft and steady save for the occasional hitch in Amelia's as some unseen pain lanced through her.

"Okay."

Something in her soul sagged, relieved. But Hadley's determination kept that feeling from bowling her over. Action always helped. They slowly made their way across the main floor, her arm tight around Amelia's waist, and to bathroom. There was a smaller one upstairs, but the one on the main floor had the big, slightly crooked countertop and scrollwork mirror and little skylight above a beautiful clawfoot tub. She'd not been in it yet, not having the time or energy after work, but now she could spoil Amelia like she'd been wanting.

"You are going to sit," Hadley said, pointing to the little chair in the corner; the one with scarred wooden legs and butter-soft velvet. An odd place to have such an elaborate chair, but she was grateful for it now.

Amelia didn't protest. It was as if all her energy was focused on simply breathing in and out, forcing herself to not shake in pain. Hadley's heart *hurt* watching her friend suffer. She helped get off heavy work boots and thick socks, and then with a silent prayer to the many, many gods she'd met in temples on her travels, Hadley pressed her thumbs into Amelia's ankles.

Amelia froze briefly, then groaned as she sank into the chair. "Hads."

"I know, babe. One thing at a time." She squeezed Amelia's knees before dashing off to her room. "I'll be right back!"

She ran, her own boots clomping. But there was no time to take them off, not when the thing she needed was so close. Her room was an explosion of color and strangeness - her own things scattered about all the decorating done by the owner. The big bed was like a dream, and the multi-hued blankets, big fluffy pillows, and soft red canopy made her feel like a queen. She knew Amelia's room housed a similar bed and for one brief moment, she stood near her bags and imagined. Imagined Amelia spread out across soft down pillows and shiny satin, her red hair curling over her shoulders. Shoulders that were bare, leading the gaze down to an artful swoop of collarbones and then lower. Something like *desire* thundered through her.

Hadley shook herself, sucked in a deep breath, and then dove into the tiny closet, hands seeking. She knew the feel of the robe she sought and when her fingers brushed against it, she grinned in triumph. It was one of her older robes, a powder blue with dancing flowers and hummingbirds arching delicately across its sky. It would look divine on Amelia and all that pale skin.

She dashed back to the bathroom and caught Amelia mid bend over the tub. "Hey, not allowed," she teased, watching as Amelia turned with guilt all over her features. "Sorry, had to find it."

She thrust the robe out and motioned Amelia behind the mango wood screen in the corner opposite the chair. "Hads..."

As swift as anything, and as daring as she'd never been before, she reached for the first button on Amelia's shirt. "Get changed. I brought you this, too." And she pressed the small flask into Amelia's other hand. "Or I can go back to tea, if you want."

Her fingers didn't shake, but it certainly felt like her *soul* did as she flicked open that single button and waited for Amelia's protest.

When her friend stayed silent, Hadley wanted to curse. Where was her friend's acerbic wit, her well-tuned and gentle deflections? But Amelia stared ahead, her gaze distant. And Hadley was forced to push away her yearning; Amelia's health came first, always. "You okay there?" she prodded, smoothing her palms over the tight line of Amelia's shoulders.

"Yeah."

"Okay. But you should get changed. I'll fill up the tub. I can see you're hurting, babe."

"Uh huh."

"Better go, unless you need me to help with something?"

Amelia looked *exhausted* when she lifted her chin, gaze pinning Hadley down. "I think I'm stuck here. Right here, on this bit of floor."

Hadley couldn't stop her smile. So she reached out to take the flask and uncap it before handing it back. "Try a bit of this. It's motivation juice."

Amelia gave the flask a sniff. "Eugh, what is that?"

"Last of the bourbon I got when I worked at that distillery last year. It'll set your throat on fire if you take more than a sip."

"Good to know." Amelia threw the flask back, gulping hard, then flipped the cap back on and handed it to Hadley. Hadley was gaping, she knew it, and Amelia chuckled. "See, you don't know *everything* about me." And then she disappeared behind the screen, robe fluttering.

The tub was half full and Hadley was poking through the wicker basket of bath salts when Amelia asked, "Are there any jasmine ones in there? I saw some rose ones but I'm not a big fan."

"Um...okay so rose, something called "Cloud Nine" that smells like...yeah, that smells like those pine tree things you hang in cars. Gross. There's a kind of cinnamon one that isn't too bad, it'd be like sitting in chai. This one's nice, it's a little softer, like candy but not as sweet. Oh, there is!" Hadley pulled the jar out as Amelia came out from behind the screen.

Hadley's first thought - really her only thought - was how much Amelia looked like a Hollywood starlet. Amelia had a round, open face with the kind of symmetrical sharpness that brought old-school beauty to mind. But in that robe (*her robe*), with her hair soft and curling over her shoulders and her perfect, pale skin, Hadley saw a redheaded Hedy Lamarr with killer curves.

She felt like she'd been punched. Hadley swayed a little on her feet, gripping the countertop with a hand. "Is that the jasmine?" Amelia asked as she approached, dipping a hand in the water to check the temperature. "Oh, that's perfect."

"Yeah. Here." Her voice was a croak and she coughed to clear it away, drawing Amelia's concerned gaze. "I'm fine. The smelly ones really smell."

"You sniffed every one, didn't you?" Amelia took the jar and began measuring out bath salts. A cloud of jasmine enveloped the room and the water turned opaque, swirling with murky blues and greens.

"Guilty." She gave Amelia a weak smile. "Now, tea?"

"No, not now." Amelia nodded at the tub. "I'll just wait for this."

Freedom lay just on the other side of the door. She didn't want to leave, but doing so meant being able to breathe again on her own. "Text me if you need anything?"

What I want to do is rub your shoulders while you sit in a tub of boiling water and try to unwind. I want to gather your hair up on top of your head and watch the loose strands cling to your neck in the humidity.

And I want to, so badly, reach into that water and massage your arms, your hands, your legs. I want to take care of you, Amelia, and somehow, even now, that scares me.

"Can you do me a favor, Hads?"

Hadley blinked. "Yeah, of course."

It wasn't even close to the brightest smile Amelia had ever graced her with, but this one felt special, somehow. "Can you pick out one of those trashy paperbacks and read it to me? I just..." Amelia's hands clenched in the robe's pockets; Hadley could see the outline of her fists. "I need to hear something other than my own thoughts right now."

She wasn't going to say something ridiculous like, "Oh, you want me to be in here with you". A little stunned, Hadley nodded and said, "Yeah, of course."

When she was free, outside the bathroom and gulping air like she'd been submerged for minutes, Hadley immediately went over to the crowded bookshelves. She let her fingers do the searching, bumping along cracked paperbacks of all different sizes, until she stopped on what looked like a more modern rom-com. Surely that would be okay; innocent enough in the first few chapters. On her way back, Hadley snagged the bottle of white wine from the fridge and hooked mismatched goblets between her fingers.

"Hey Ames, you decent?" she called through the closed bathroom door.

"I'm naked in a tub, Hadley."

She was *not* going to try to out-quip her friend. She wasn't. "Yeah and I have wine and a trashy book, so I win."

Dammit.

Amelia's chuckle was almost a soft purr. "You dork, get in here."

The armchair had moved from the corner (*dammit Amelia, don't move furniture*), where Hadley would have only been able to see the back of Amelia's head, to facing the tub. So they had to face each other. Candles flickered in the cozy warmth of the room. Soft moonlight filtered in through the window on the opposite wall, giving Hadley a silvery path to follow into the room. "Are you sure?"

Arms resting on the tub's rolled edge, hair piled high on top of her head, her friend looked like some kind princess or wealthy lady. Her wide brown eyes were half-lidded, expression almost sleepy, and Hadley blew out a silent breath at seeing her friend relaxed. "Positive. Read to me?"

And what else could Hadley do but pour them wine and take up her spot in the chair? Amelia sniffed her wine then sipped it, expression melting even further into untethered pleasure. "Good?" Hadley asked, following suit. "Oh, shit. That is good. I thought I was picking a stinker but damn."

"You thought wine from the store would be bad?" Amelia scoffed but her lips had a certain curl to them; one Hadley knew well. "I never."

"Well, to be fair, white isn't my usual."

"Too true." Amelia leaned her head back with a sigh. "I don't know the last time I saw you drink white wine, actually."

There was a memory from the depths of their friendship. "Remember Jamal's barbecue, about five years ago?"

Amelia's eyes shot open and she started to laugh. "Oh *fuck*, that's right! And Jack started passing around that pitcher of white sangria."

"We got so drunk. And I swore to never, ever again drink white wine of any kind." Hadley raised her glass and peered at the shimmering golden liquid. "And here we are."

Amelia let out a snort. "I'm a bad influence, apparently."

"It was my choice to grab this wine."

"True."

From her spot in the tub - her very vulnerable spot - Amelia gave her a look that sent a pleasant shiver down Hadley's spine. She had to be imagining it, the hopeful fever dream of the long unrequited. But she swore that look scraped over her with a purpose, one that rattled her bones. She had to push it aside, ignore it. Sink deeper into the chair, sip her wine, then start reading the book.

Hadley held the book up so Amelia could see the cover. "Any objections?"

But Amelia's eyes were closed, the glass of wine half empty but set aside. She flicked a hand in Hadley's direction. Water drops flew in an arc. "I trust your judgment."

If Hadley kept drinking wine at a similar pace, things would start to get interesting around page five. Forcing herself to put the wine glass down, she cracked open the book and saw a few names scribbled on the inside cover. Remnants of the other people, the other hands, that had touched the book, while the worn edges proved it had been read. Hopefully they'd enjoyed it.

She took a deep breath and started to read to Amelia. It was one of those meet-cute books, full of fluff and good feelings, and it made for easy narrating. Settling into the story was like wrapping up in a blanket and Hadley found herself enjoying the domesticity of both the book and the moment she and Amelia were caught in. It had been a long time since she'd read out loud to her friend, but it was a strange kind of muscle memory that sprang to life, making the pages fly by.

Only when Amelia stirred with a wince did Hadley stop. "Ames?"

"My shoulder. Where I hit it on the ground." She shifted again, the water sloshing. "I'll be a gorgeous shade of blue and green tomorrow, I'm guessing."

Hadley was on her feet immediately. "Do you have any balm or anything we can put on it?"

Amelia looked away. "No. I ran out and forgot to buy more."

"Ames." Hadley went over to the tub and kneeled down so they were eye to eye. Once Amelia turned back to her. "I can run out and get something. What do you need?"

"It's late, the pharmacy will be closed."

"Then I'll find a twenty-four hour one."

"I'm fine."

"You're not and you know it. And I know it." *And I love you and I want to help you so quit being so goddamn stubborn.*

Amelia shook her head. A loose spiral of red hair fell out of her bun and stuck to her neck. Hadley averted her eyes as if it were something far more scandalous. "Really. The bath is actually helping instead of making me bored and forcing me out before the heat has a chance to work."

Well, shit. Hadley had to laugh at that. "You get bored in the bath?" She was just happy for the distraction. "It's...it's a chance to be still and quiet and just *be*."

"Exactly." Now Amelia was the one looking away, down at pruney hands she pulled up from the water. "Too much time to think."

"Oh." She stared hard at her friend, worry now a slowly growing ball of lead in her belly. "Hey. What's going on?"

Amelia shrugged, then winced, hissing as her shoulder pulled. Hadley immediately reached out, then checked herself. If Amelia needed her help, she'd ask. She'd learned that a long time ago and tried very hard not to stomp on those boundaries. "It's been stressful," Amelia admitted. "No surprise, I'm sure. But it's been..."

A long pause hung between. Then slowly, carefully, Hadley put her hand on Amelia's smooth forearm. She squeezed it gently and

Amelia's shoulders instantly pulled away from her ears. "Do you want me to rub your arms or your hands?"

Please don't pull away. Please don't pull away.

"My shoulders, maybe?"

Hadley nearly went limp with relief. But for Amelia's sake — and hers, honestly — she had to keep up the quips. Be *Hadley*, be Amelia's best friend and always-there-human. "Yeah, of course. Just let me know when you're out of the bath and I can help."

Amelia blinked. Looked away. Bit her lip. Looked back. By the time Hadley registered all that, Amelia's cheeks were redder. "Would now be okay? The water's still hot and I don't want to get out and I'm probably more relaxed -"

Hadley slid her grip down and squeezed Amelia's hand, interlacing their fingers. "Say no more."

There was a footstool in the corner, so Hadley brought it and more towels over. Some part of her was secretly more at ease now that she was seated behind Amelia and not staring at wide brown eyes or splashes of freckles across a round face and upper chest. Temptation lay there. It was ground on which she dared not tread, though in reality she knew that she should just confess. Say something, anything, to tell Amelia how she felt. But like the age old story, fear of losing her best friend won out every single time.

A terrible, horrible, bittersweet thing.

As Hadley stared at Amelia's soft skin and rounded shoulders, she sighed. Then got to work; pulled up her hair, tightened the messy loop she strung it into, and then put her hands on Amelia's biceps. "Ready?"

"Yes."

She'd done this before, maybe dozens of times in the past. This one was different. This time scared her. She was raw from the torrent of emotions; from the gripping, needy, clawing thing that was her love. Hadley's eyes burned as she leaned forward to rest her forehead on the back of Amelia's head. She felt her friend's deep breath, the way her shoulders sank that final, precious inch.

Relaxed. Easy. Slow. Quiet.

Her Amelia finally letting go, letting Hadley be the one to take her there. That yearning in her soul rushed forward, ready to claim, so convinced it was finally free to exclaim to the world how much she loved this person. How she ached with it.

All she could do was confess.

Hadley pressed her fingers into Amelia's shoulders, desperate to brand the memory of that touch into her brain. Like preserving flowers between the pages of a book. Forever embalmed, then set aside.

She couldn't keep doing this. Couldn't keep torturing herself.

"I love you," she whispered.

CHAPTER FIVE

There was no stopping the tears that dripped into her bathwater. Amelia knew Hadley couldn't see her but somehow that didn't matter in the moment. Some part of her wanted; wanted Hadley to see the tears, the twisted frown, the sadness and love swimming in her eyes.

Because Hadley's "I love you" devastated her.

It shattered her reality, her solid wall built on doubts and fears. The wall meant to protect her heart and hide the one secret she'd never, ever tell.

But Hadley *loved her*.

Her inhale trembled as she sought to regain some kind of balance. And those warm fingers, slippery from the bath oils, stilled on her shoulders. "Ames?"

The tears still fell. Her breath still shook. But she couldn't answer. She tried to convince herself she didn't know *how* but Amelia knew that was cowardly.

She loved Hadley. Always had, and always would. And now...

"Ames, you're scaring me." The sound of wood creaking hit her and then Hadley was on her right, staring at her over the lip of the tub. "What hurts? What do you need -"

"Hadley."

Hadley's gaze shot up to meet hers, and Amelia took the chance to lean forward. She was distantly aware of her nudity, her vulnerability. Of the closeness of Hadley's warmth and scent, how easily she could twist her fingers into those waves or run fingertips across that rounded jaw. She knew all of that. "I'm sorry," she whispered. It was all she could force out against the weight like a semi truck on her chest.

It was too much. *Overwhelmed* didn't cover the depth of what she was feeling, how it crashed over her, rolled her around until her world had no up or down, left or right. She saw Hadley swallow hard, tracked the movement of her throat and itched to follow the path with a touch. "Sorry for what?"

Amelia's frown deepened. "That I got hurt. I was careless. I was in such a rush and that put it on you and that's so unfair. I know better. But I can't just...sit around and let everyone do everything for me. But when you're here, it's like..." Hadley watched her with caution and care and it hurt. So much, too much. "It's like I forget when you're gone. When you come back, I mean. Because you fill in the holes. And then I do something stupid and get hurt, and I worry I'm taking advantage of you."

"Wait, what?" Instantly Hadley was grabbing her hand, squeezing it hard. "Never. Never ever ever." That lovely voice, a crooner's melody bound in silk, hardened. "You are never a burden. Not to me, not to anyone. And if anyone has ever made you feel that way, point me to them. I'll get the knives."

"Hads." The tears drying on her face were starting to feel tacky but there was no reality in which she let go of Hadley.

"No, I'm serious." Hadley gave her hand a final squeeze and let go. "Because you do so fucking much and it's not *fair* that anyone has made you feel like that. You can't help your body, and hell, I just -" Hadley stopped herself abruptly and looked away. "I know you've been through it over the years," she finally said, arctic tone now melted . "Can I admit something?" Breath caught somewhere between her lungs and throat, Amelia nodded. "I had a long flight over and I was trying to sleep and nothing was working. Not even listening to that rain soundtrack you gave me. So I'm lying there staring at the ceiling, wondering what was next. Cause there's usually something. But all I could think about was this new place and the new business and how in the middle of all of the newness, there would be you. So it didn't matter what was next because I'd be with you."

Her Hadley. *Hers.*

Amelia choked out a watery laugh. "I think you're definitely stuck now. Plus, there's a big garden here you know I'll kill by looking at it wrong, and Mr. Buttons goes to you first. I think you've been adopted."

That got Amelia the laugh she'd been hoping for. The one she really needed, because otherwise the pressure of what she'd nearly done would have burst out from her. "Okay but I'm still making him that vest. I already got the pieces cut."

Amelia really did love this woman. For her, there was no one else. "He'll look adorable. You better start making more though. I might need to display them in the shop."

Hadley beamed at her.

"Purple or blue?"

"Hmm?"

Hadley held up two tablecloths. The purple was a thick purple velvet that needed to be hemmed properly. And the blue was so dark it looked almost black, but it would need weights sewn in to keep it from slipping. "I'm undecided. You're a decider. Help."

Amelia gave the frame by her right shoulder a nudge to center it. When Hadley sent her the thumbs up, her friend turned that full focus onto her. "The blue."

"Oh, very decisive."

"You asked."

She smiled. "I did. So I'm going to put this upstairs and water the plants."

Amelia wiggled the hammer in her hand. "Go forth and cleanse the air, my friend."

That made her wrinkle her nose. "You'd need a lot of plants up there to get all the alcohol out of the air."

Amelia's answer was a snort and an eye roll before turning back to the various decorations left to hang up. Hadley took her time fussing with the little corner nook Amelia had given her for her dog and cat sweaters to sell and the tarot readings she'd be doing. The readings were just for fun, but she was already devising a calendar of events; one at Amelia's behest, of course. But time alone meant her mind wandered, and it never wandered more than when she was absorbed in a calming task like sewing or tending to plants.

She looked over a little succulent that she'd repotted last week and sighed. The wall of various pots and jars, all salvaged from the local recycling center, glinted in the soft afternoon light that poured in from the skylights. The plants were thriving in this spot, just like she figured they would. And in the evening, their leaves shone softly as the pendant lights over the bar and tables flickered on. It was a magical spot, a little indoor garden with wine and conversation and she couldn't wait to watch it flourish. To watch Amelia flourish.

The bathroom, the confessions, and ultimately Amelia asking her to move in had been three days ago. Three *days*. It had felt like forever in the best kind of way. She went to sleep with the creaking of trees humming lullabies, occasionally backed up by soft drumming rain. They made coffee to-go at home, said goodbye to Mr. Buttons if he was around, and then drove Amelia's little hatchback into Breakwater to park behind the store and start their day. It was *routine*, it was *normal*.

For Hadley, it was heaven.

Maybe age was the real burden here, so eager to show Hadley what she'd been missing all those years bouncing around the planet. It sounded nice, the life of a wandering backpacker who went from city to city, breathing in oceans and markets and drinking in cafes. But sustaining that got harder each time she had to leave Amelia.

Because she'd been leaving home every time, and every time it hurt more.

There had been a moment that night, when she'd whispered her secret into the humid air and the soft skin of Amelia's back; a moment she'd thought would turn into something desperately wanted but nearly unthinkable. But then they'd gone back to that same old balance. It was a good balance, made of solid rock and all the troubles and turmoil and celebrations any life went through. And Hadley was used to loving from afar, or as it was now, as close as she could get. Nothing — *nothing* — could drive her from Amelia. She'd lived with her love buried deep for years. One slip up, one moment of weakness, wouldn't change that.

From downstairs, the shop bell dinged. "My staff are coming in for training," Amelia yelled from below. "You good up there?"

"All good!" Hadley spritzed a couple of orchids.

"Good if I send up the new sommelier?"

"Yep!"

There were two part-time sommeliers in training whom she'd already met. But apparently this new person had popped up on Amelia's radar recently and they'd chatted, which had quickly turned into an interview and then a job. Hadley wasn't good at any of that wine tasting stuff and admired Amelia's rarefied taste buds, but she would admit to zoning out when Amelia found another wine nerd to talk shop with.

"You must be Hadley."

The curly-haired man standing at the top of the stairs was smiling at her with an open friendliness that instantly made Hadley smile back. She could tell right away he was one of those easy chatters, the kind who drew people in with an affable air and calm demeanor. "Yeah, hey. Nice to meet you..."

He took her proffered hand and gave it a firm shake. "Larsen." As he stepped back, Larsen's gaze swung across the plant and light filled space. "This is so cool! I got to see up here when I met with Amelia last week but it's like the jungle grew overnight. Do you take care of all of these?"

Pride swelled in her chest. "Yeah, it's kind of my 'thing'. So you never have to worry about them."

Larsen chuckled. "Good cause me and plants are like oil and water. Always ends badly."

Yep, she instantly liked him. Upfront without being too forthright, friendly and laid-back. It helped that he was wearing the kind of clothes she personally gravitated toward; comfortable but funky, full of color and patterns. His boots were heeled and embroidered in burnt orange and crimson, and Larsen was wearing a matching orange jacket. His dark red shirt, black jeans, and layers of silver necklaces were exactly right. "Good thing you have killer fashion sense, makes up for the plant murder," she joked. Larsen laughed and it brightened his dark brown eyes. "So, checking out the space again?"

Larsen's smile grew. "Thanks. Usually the colors get some looks but I like them and that's all that matters. And yeah, I'm getting the wine bar set up for the big opening night. Amelia and I mocked up a plan, but I gotta touch things to get them all settled out in my mind. If that makes sense."

Larsen navigated through the snaking line of two and four seater bistro tables, the ones Hadley had helped Amelia pick out before she arrived in Breakwater. As he began to work behind the bar, Hadley saw how confidently he moved, how serious he took the work. Amelia had, again, chosen well. She just had a knack for knowing people and where they'd best perform or how to make good use of their talents. An idea hit her, one that had her stomach tumbling with excitement. Amelia deserved someone who could take care of her, and Hadley wanted to show her all the ways she could be good to her.

"Hey so wine," Hadley said as she went over to the big curved bar and plonked down on a stool. She dropped her voice as Larsen looked up at her. "Let's say I know nothing about it. But I want to learn. Where do I start?"

"I love newbies." Larsen pulled two bottles off the floor to ceiling rack behind the bar and set them down. "Let's start with some easy stuff."

When Amelia walked into the cottage with grocery bags over her shoulder, she was greeted by an enthusiastic Mr. Buttons wearing a dark turquoise vest. "Look at you," she crooned, shifting the bags off her arm and to the floor. Mr. Buttons gave her a headbutt and several soft meows. "I see you got new clothes. You look great, sir."

"Hey!" Hadley swung into view. "Do you like his vest? He wasn't even a little mad when I put it on him. Sat like a champ."

"Uh, Hads?"

"Yeah?"

Amelia motioned to her friend. And the bright yellow apron she was wearing; the apron that complemented the blue scarf holding up the pile of wavy brown hair on top of her head. "What's going on?"

She expected an impish grin, one Hadley had cultivated over years of convincing people to go her way. But Hadley sobered, her high cheekbones standing out in sharp relief as she grew serious. "Dinner. A proper dinner. Not that I don't love cooking together but uh..." She trailed off, slipping her gaze away from Amelia's. Something pinched in Amelia's heart. The urge to ask what was really going on - what was *wrong* - nearly had her interrupting Hadley. "We've been working our asses off and I was determined to make good use of the bit of extra time I had this afternoon. Since *someone* shooed me out of the store two hours before they even thought about leaving."

"I wondered why you didn't fight me on that."

"Well, come see!"

Hadley scooped up the grocery bags and marched her into the kitchen, where the stove was packed with simmering pots and pans and the scent of fresh herbs and olive oil wove through the air. Mr. Buttons took up his usual spot in a nearby armchair to watch. "It's not fancy," Hadley said as she started stirring a pot. "But I made chicken meatballs and spaghetti squash with chickpea salad. Oh! And dessert!

Strawberry tarts with…" She held up a spoon coated in a thick red sauce. "Pureed lemon-strawberry sauce."

The spoon was held out in offering, Hadley's expression expectant. Amelia reached for the spoon but, at the last moment, switched up her play. Hadley was being Hadley, but that didn't mean she had to be boring old Amelia. If they were both going to dance around this…thing between them, maybe she should make the first attempt. They'd been flirty before, friendly-type things that included touching and hugs and teasing words. But never this. Never this strange, warm closeness that Amelia felt bubble up in her chest.

When Amelia closed her lips over the spoon, the flash of surprise in Hadley's eyes was payment enough. But the fact that the sauce was delicious helped, too. "That is so good," she groaned, not at all trying to inject pleasure into her voice. It happened naturally. "Jesus, Hads. I knew you could cook but wow."

"Oh! Okay well…" For a long moment, her best friend looked both happy and a little lost all at the same time. It was an adorable expression, once that had her scrunching her freckled nose and sending her gaze darting about until it landed on a bubbling pot. "I'm glad you like it."

"I love it."

The heat from the stove wasn't the only thing sending color into Hadley's cheeks. A rush of pride nearly had Amelia grinning. *Poker face. Poker face. Don't give up the game yet.*

"Okay well, you sit," Hadley said as she bustled into the little pantry, the one done up in faded wallpaper dotted with tiny yellow flowers and the scent of flour and sugar. "I got us drinks, too."

"You didn't have to do all this, you know."

"No, I didn't. I wanted to."

How many times had she heard that over the years? Hadley had a thing for spoiling people and Amelia had been the recipient a countless number of times of that thoughtful kindness. Given the number of herbs around the kitchen, Amelia figured the drinks were some kind of tea Hadley had blended herself.

She was not expecting a tasting board of small wine glasses. And Hadley's nervous grin said a lot. "So! Your new sommelier, Larsen? Super nice guy, Ames. Good job. But he showed me some stuff about wine and I thought it might be nice for you to be treated instead of being the one always teaching others about it."

Amelia stared down at the tasting board and couldn't stop the delighted laughter bubbling up from within. "You picked out wine?"

"I did!" Hadley looked utterly pleased. "With Larsen's help, of course."

Hadley talked her through the five selections; all reds, from sweet to dry and then a blend at the end. "I've not had any of these," Amelia marveled, admiring the dark plum color of a cabernet sauvignon.

"That's what I was hoping for."

When Amelia looked up at her friend, Hadley was shining with giddy joy and warm satisfaction. It all made Amelia's heart sing and her lungs ache and her stomach twist into an impossible knot of *wanting*. Hadley had always been beautiful, and she was never more full of spirit when she was helping others. But standing in the kitchen of their little rented cottage, the scent of a good home cooked meal floating around them, Amelia felt all sorts of undone. Even more than three days ago in the bath. Wrestling with her own feelings was difficult on the best of days. She was used to shoving the strongest of them into some dark corner and ignoring them for the sake of accomplishing a task. *Practical Amelia*. Head down, mind churning, hands busy. But

Hadley upended all of that. Hadley made her pause to enjoy things, to slow down, to *breathe.*

And breathing Hadley in right now was doing something to her gut in a way that Amelia had come to recognize as desire. More than raw lust, but the need to take and give and make Hadley hers. And that confused her practicality, her logic; it messed with her tidy to-do list and decades of friendship. But Hadley had always done that, spun her round until her head and her heart were one. So what was different now?

Hadley reading to her, making her tea. Hadley running her a bath, making sure her hands weren't too swollen or numb by rubbing them with her own. The soft waves of her long brown hair tumbling from those jewel-hued scarves she always wore. Hadley's freckles and adorable nose and the architecturally stunning slope of her collarbones. The achingly sweet way she cared for everyone around her.

Hadley slicking her skin with oil and whispering confessions into her shoulder blades.

Hadley loved her. That was the difference. And now she knew and it burned.

But Amelia didn't have to idly sit by anymore. Not now. Maybe it would all fall apart. Maybe it wouldn't.

Hadley *loved* her. Truly. In a way that went beyond their years and years of friendship and trust and all the memories they'd built with rope ladders and notes in glitter pen and books read under the shade of an old oak tree. Those memories lived in Amelia and she cherished every single one. But all that time spent worrying about what would happen if she admitted how badly she wanted Hadley, and how much she loved her? Now it didn't seem so important. Things felt *different*. They felt *right*. And if she was going to work this out, and truly talk to

Hadley about how she felt, she'd need to find a way to make it special. For her. For Hadley.

For *them*.

CHAPTER SIX

S omething was different about Amelia. Sure, Hadley could tell she was nervous as the store opening approached. They all were thrumming with that heady excitement that also came with stomach butterflies and cold sweats, but she'd been through a few big deals like this. Nothing *quite* this important, as it was Amelia's store. But when one of the wait staff dropped a tray this afternoon, the sound echoing off exposed brick and glass, several employees had jumped at least six feet in the air. Amelia had been behind the main floor bar, helping Larsen write up the opening night tasting menus, and when Hadley turned to check on them, she locked eyes with her friend. Ames was pale enough but that blast of noise must have split her frayed nerves.

As Amelia excused herself and ducked into the service hallway, Hadley tossed her clipboard onto a table and followed. She waited until they were mostly out of earshot before saying Amelia's name once.

"I just need a minute," Amelia muttered as she rattled the doorknob to her office. Her left hand went to her chest and Hadley saw her pluck up the key she'd gifted Amelia and rub it between her thumb and forefinger. She'd been doing that a lot lately.

Hadley stayed back a few paces, not wanting to crowd. "Do you need me to keep working out on the floor?"

Amelia hesitated, sighed. Then leaned her forehead on the door and let her arms drop. "No. Stay." She turned her head. "Please."

Hadley slipped in beside her and opened the door. They took up their usual spots in Amelia's bright, cheery office, with her flopped on the little couch in the corner and Amelia plopping down hard in her cushy desk chair. The chair was custom made and meant to help support her spine and shoulders. It looked like the Stay Puft Man's brother, all poofy and plush, and it never failed to make her grin.

"You're laughing at my chair again." Amelia's pout was epic but also mostly fake. "Mean."

"Me? Never." Hadley grabbed for one of the throw pillows and shoved it under her head. "I keep making us delicious dinners. I made Mr. Buttons three vests this week and you said they made you happy!"

"People are going to think he's the shop cat," she replied, not raising her head from her curled fist. "Maybe we need a shop cat."

"We need a shop cat." No question in her mind, and Hadley could picture a fluffy rescue sporting all the best vests and little coats. She'd definitely need more fabric.

The half-lidded gaze focused on her sharpened. Hadley suddenly felt as though Amelia was really looking *at* her. She tried not to squirm. "Take your hair down for me?"

"What?"

Amelia drew a lazy circle in the air, centered around Hadley's face. "I never see it down except before you go to bed. It's so pretty. Remember when we tried to French braid each other's hair in third grade?"

Hadley winced. "Oooh don't remind me. I still hate curling irons to this day."

Amelia's snort was a thing of beauty. "Which one of us thought French braids required frying our hair with your mom's curling iron?"

"I thought you had to curl each section first! And the curling iron was weirdly heavy and..."

"And I went into fourth grade with a pixie cut."

"Sorry, babe."

"I know." Amelia shifted in her chair, arms now draped elegantly over the arm rests, legs parted slightly as she let the padding cushion her body. It was very hard not to stare at the way Amelia's favorite worn black jeans hugged her strong thighs. She'd worked hard over the years to build her strength; which made it difficult for Hadley not to acknowledge how much that work had paid off.

Amelia's throaty purr of words soon startled Hadley out of her daydreams. "Make it up to me by taking your hair down."

There was a command in Amelia's voice. Soft but unmistakable. Firm but not unyielding. Something in Hadley wanted to drop to its knees before her. "Okay." Proud her hands were steady, Hadley reached up and undid the knot at the back of her head. The ends of the dark yellow scarf tickled her neck while she pulled the few pins from her hair. Her hair was thick and heavy and a pain in the ass but cutting it beyond a trim never felt right. And in this moment, Hadley was more than thankful she'd waved away the temptation to cut it right before coming to Breakwater.

Because the way Amelia was looking at her made Hadley's heart race.

She paused for only a moment, but in that flicker of time, Hadley swore the air between them sizzled.

What was going on? Was...was Amelia flirting with her?

Well, shit.

And she let her hair drop. In Hadley's mind, it did some sexy tumbling thing and made her look beautiful and perfect and Amelia would rush to her and kiss her senseless. But what she got was even better.

A deep intake of breath. A sigh. And Amelia slid further down into her chair, legs spread wider, fingers gripping the armrests. She looked powerful, exacting. Dominant. A shiver ran down Hadley's spine. "Better?" Hadley asked, knowing her voice was trembling.

"Much." Amelia got to her feet and crossed the small space between them to pick up the scarf from Hadley's lap. It dangled from her fingers, its tassels brushing Hadley's cheek. "This is such a pretty color on you, this goldenrod yellow. I don't know another person who pulls it off like you do."

"Thanks."

Before she could mentally slap herself for the wobble in her voice, Amelia chuckled and laid the scarf over Hadley's shoulder. "Will you let me brush this tonight? I miss playing with your hair."

Heat rushed through her. The urge to squirm in her seat was strong. *Steady. Steady.* "You can play with it now." *You can play with me now, too. Ah, hells. Don't think like that. Not now.*

"I'd love to." With the lightest touch, Amelia ran her fingers over the ends of Hadley's hair, where it rested against her bicep. Hadley swore that touch went through her entire body, a sweet thing that tightened the coil in her gut. Or maybe that tightening was because of the raw emotion on Amelia's face.

Maybe she was remembering, too; remembering all the sleepovers and homework assignments agonized over, and all the concerts and video game tournaments and making themselves sick on crappy pizza and soda. Remembering the later years, separating to go to college and then coming back together when Hadley dropped out to travel. Remembering seeing a play at The Globe and walking the cliffs in Scotland. Napping together in the afternoon while in Spain, the tiny home they rented flooded with soft sunlight blocked only by the fine white mesh around the bed. Every meal, every glass of wine, every late night, every phone call. Remembered over and over again, a story of time and space and friendship and adoration. Fueled by love.

"So pretty," Amelia murmured. Something in her eyes flashed when Hadley fought back a shiver. "Are you okay?"

Hadley swallowed hard. How could she answer that truthfully? Rustling around for her courage was like digging through a haystack and she *couldn't*. It wasn't there for her to pluck out and use, to buoy the words up and out of her throat.

Someone knocked at the door.

"Hey, Amelia? There's a delivery guy out here for you with a pretty big box. You gotta sign for it."

Amelia stepped back and Hadley could breathe again. But just barely. "I'll be right out, Larsen. Thank you."

"Sure thing."

Larsen's footsteps retreated down the hallway. "Ames," Hadley croaked, reaching for her. There was no resistance anymore; only a truth she'd already whispered into Amelia's shoulders and one she needed to see echoed in her best friend. Hadley could taste it lingering in the air, but she needed to *hear it.*

And then she realized what was in the box the delivery guy was holding. Hadley bolted up out of her seat, somewhat thankful for the distraction even as her heart pounded in her ears. She grabbed Amelia's hand and raced them down the hall, eager for the reveal.

Ten people stood at the main bar of Classy Corks and admired the hand-carved wooden plaque now hanging behind the bar. Amelia was still in shock over Hadley's gift, and she couldn't stop running her fingers over the perfect curves of the carved goblet decorated with swirling vines and plump grapes. "What am I supposed to do with you?" she whispered as Hadley edged closer.

Hadley's pretty lips twisted into a pleased smirk. "Whatever you want," she teased. There was a note of something darker in her friend's voice. Was Hadley tuned into Amelia's little game? She hadn't meant to lure her in so quickly, not really; but Hadley was wily and smart and somehow, Amelia wasn't surprised at her teasing.

She was surprised at the warm, firm hand suddenly in the small of her back. Supportive. Not pushing or pressing, but present. Sensation rippled through Amelia's body, slinking under her skin, making her fingers twitch against the wood.

"Everyone's staring," Hadley said softly.

"Then ...you know what?" Amelia turned to face her employees. "Fuck it. Who wants wine?"

A cheer went up.

As everyone took up stools at the bar and Sara ran off to get snacks and Larsen pulled down some decent bottles, Amelia found herself steered out of view, into the corner under the stairs. Her back was against the wall. Hadley was close. *Too close. Not enough. Not nearly enough.* "Who are you and what did you do with my Amelia?" Hadley asked, breathless excitement in her voice. Her hands were at her sides but they were curled into loose fists. And Amelia realized Hadley had never put her hair back up. That thick tangle begged for her touch. It made her ache in a way that sent lust blooming through her.

"I'm on the other side of thirty-five, it's been a long week, and I need a break," she admitted. Easier to say that than beg Hadley to come closer so she could wrap her fingers in that hair. She ran her fingers over the key hanging from her neck.

Hadley's gaze went to her hand. And her neck. And that key. "What's age got to do with it, babe?"

"I'm feeling every bit my age. All thirty-seven years of it. Add ten for the chronic pain and yeah. I just need to...to..."

To kiss you. To hold you so close I can't figure out where we start or end and it won't matter because we'll share breath like that's the only way we can live. I'll run my tongue up your neck and feel you sigh and that will be the end of me. Because no matter how deep our connection, something in me needs to feel you.

"I just need to breathe," Amelia said lamely. "I knew this would be a ton of work but you think oh, I've got employees, that's all the more hands. But the weight of it is a lot some days."

"Staggering."

"Intensely so."

Understanding crackled between them. Finally, Hadley gave her a slow nod and backed up a few steps. "I get it. I'm sorry. I shouldn't have questioned."

"You're looking out for me."

And for some reason, that statement, as true as it was, made Hadley frown. "Yeah. Yeah, of course."

That frown stayed with Amelia through the rest of the day, far into evening as they reheated leftovers and made tea. Some nights Hadley was as tired as she, but tonight felt heavier. Disappointment sat thick on Amelia's tongue and it left her unable to do much other than listen to the rattle and purr of the sewing machine beside her while she read and scratched Mr. Buttons behind the ears.

Amelia was the first to cave. "I'm beat," she said, standing up to let Mr. Buttons curl up in her seat. "Don't kill your eyes, Hads."

Hadley grinned at her and the world righted a little bit. "Nah, just finishing this one up because I promised Irene, that lady with the big poodle, that I'd bring it by this weekend." She held up a toddler-sized bright blue corduroy vest with chunky silver buttons. "And the inside...voila!" She turned it so Amelia could see inside of the vest was patterned cotton; dove gray with blueberries and tiny white flowers.

"Okay, that's adorable. Where the hell did you find strawberry patterned fabric?"

"My secret! No! You won't make me give it up."

Amelia snorted and rolled her eyes playfully at Hadley's antics. The cowardly part of her was glad to have regular old Hadley back. Everything else in her missed flirty Hadley, testing her with subtle looks and the way she left her hair down. A tease. It really was that, right?

When that old monster *doubt* crept back in, Amelia figured it was best to go to bed and let her mind settle, give herself a chance to shore up the stitch lines in her heart. She left Mr. Buttons purring and Hadley sewing and trundled off to bed. She didn't even remember dropping onto the mattress, but the crash that woke her in the night, in the dark, had Amelia scrambling for normality.

"Shit," she said into the empty, chilly air of her room. Rain lashed at the windows and jagged lines of lightning made her blink. Thunder shook the house.

"Ames?"

Oh Hadley.

"Yeah, come in."

Hadley was swaddled in a blanket from head to ankle, her eyes huge in the shadows of her makeshift hood. She looked small and scared and Amelia never gave it a second thought. "Sorry, I just..."

"Hey, it's okay." She yanked back her blankets and moved to the right. "Get in."

The roof of Hadley's childhood home had caved in when she was ten; hit by a tree downed in a horrible storm. Thankfully no one had been hurt, but it had come close to her bedroom and since then, storms required anxiety meds and tea and a quiet place in which to hunker down. But out here, near wilderness and in an old cottage that creaked and groaned, Hadley was likely reliving that night. Amelia's heart clenched as Hadley rolled herself into bed but held back on curling close. "Come on, you," she said softly, tugging on the blanket Hadley clutched. "I promise it's okay."

"I'm so sorry."

"Don't be. Your fear is justified and even if it didn't have an anchor in something that had occurred, it wouldn't matter." Amelia managed to tug the blanket from Hadley's hands and pull the end over her legs; they were sharing space but weren't close enough for her liking. "You want to be the big spoon or little spoon?"

Hadley's laugh was watery, but she said, "Little spoon. I need your strong arms around me."

Amelia bit back a smile and let Hadley shift around. Getting comfortable - and extricated from the various blankets - took a minute, but she soon had an armful of her best friend. Curled up close, their bodies molded together. Hadley's soft, jasmine-scented hair tickling her nose. Nothing could have made her move. Not a storm, not an earthquake, not the frantic, traitorous beating of her heart.

Especially not when she got up the courage to ask what weighed on her, with hope heavy on her tongue. "Hey Hadley?"

"Hmm?"

"Better?"

"Yeah." A pause. "Thank you."

"Always." Amelia snuggled closer. Took a deep breath. "Hadley?"

"Yeah?"

"You know…"

Hadley turned, shifting until she could look at Amelia in the thick dark of the room. "You okay?"

"I should be asking you that."

"You have been. My turn."

"I'm okay." She looked away. "That's a lie. I'm scared." She sucked in a deep breath, steadied her voice and her hands, and said, "Cause if I tell you I know you love me and I love you, too, what the hell happens after that?"

CHAPTER SEVEN

O^{h.}

That's what that felt like.

To hear those words. To feel her hands on my face. Her scent every-where; the prickly pear lotion on her skin, the way the sheets smelled like her. The sheets I have my face pressed into while I stare my best friend in the eyes during a storm. After she just said, "I love you."

Hadley had played this scene out before, many times, in her imagi-nation. Mostly when she was feeling a certain lonely kind of way after leaving Amelia and flying off to another place, another country. In one version, she got up the nerve to tell Amelia during a candlelit dinner in a garden, as night settled around them and the air grew humid and fragrant. In another, she was reading while Amelia napped, while the fire popped and crackled. Amelia would sit up, blink sleepily at her, and then they'd kiss. No words, just a kiss. *The* kiss.

And now, with Amelia so close and warm, Hadley heard those words, that confession, and reacted. Because her gut and her soul and every little nerve in her body knew Amelia was her first, best, only love. And because she wanted it; she wanted it so badly it sang in her body. A perfect melody.

The first brush of her lips against Amelia's made her shiver. In some strange way, they were just lips. But then her brain caught up with reality and Hadley knew. These were *Amelia's* lips and they were in

Amelia's bed, buried under blankets while a storm raged and the house rattled and she felt that tug in her chest, in her belly.

"I love you," Hadley whispered, barely able to keep the tears in check. "I've always loved you. Ames..."

Amelia cut her off with another kiss, this one sending shivers through her body. *Shit, where should I put my hands? Here, on Amelia's shoulder. No, no. I have to touch her face, get my fingertips under that sharp jaw where freckles hide in the dark hollows.*

The moment she touched Amelia's face, it felt like the room froze. Amelia gasped, the sound a rustle in the darkness. "Ames?"

"I'm good. I'm good." Amelia's fingers ran through Hadley's hair, gentle but present. Like she could have ignored the touch, as keyed up as she was right now. "I've wanted to do that for *so long*. Hadley." Amelia's forehead was pressed into hers, their lips so close and yet it felt like miles. "Hadley. Shit. Shit."

Sourness spiked the joy coursing through her. "You don't regret -"

"No. Absolutely not. Never." The sourness left her belly and Hadley was floating once more. "Hadley. *I love you.* I always have." Amelia's touch on her cheek was so sweet, so soft.

"I thought....gods. Ames."

"You thought what?"

Her next words were choked, both with emotion and laughter. "I thought something had shifted recently. You've been...flirty. The office?"

"Hmmm, yeah." Amelia laughed and the velvet darkness of that sound slipped right through Hadley. It made her flushed, that sound. "I don't know what came over me."

"I do!" She shoved playfully at Amelia's shoulder, but followed it up with a kiss. Brief, intense. Her tongue in Amelia's mouth, coaxing soft noises out of her. Running her hand down Amelia's arm. Linking their fingers together. "I do," she repeated, quieter now. "The other side of you. The Amelia I know that's a powder keg with the world's longest fuse."

"That's me, huh?" Amelia's kiss to her mouth just missed, catching the corner of Hadley's lips. "You are the only person who really knows that side. Because I'm safe with you."

"Always." Her throat was closing up again, swelled with the tsunami of feelings and understandings.

"Still worried about the storm?" Amelia's hand was on her hip now. *Oh gods.*

"No." The lightning outside had dimmed but rain pummeled the roof. The rain she could deal with. "But it's still going. And I want to hear you say it again."

"Hmmm, I bet."

"Tease."

Amelia kissed her once more and Hadley melted. "I love you," Amelia whispered against her mouth. "So much."

"I love you. Can't stand how much."

"Stay with me."

"Yes."

She fell asleep in Amelia's arms, listening to her best friend breathe.

Amelia had pictured something epic. Some fanciful, grand declaration of love; sweeping Hadley off her feet and making her feel so seen, so adored, that her friend would fall into her arms and the world would right itself.

But their lives weren't storybooks or movies. Things were always messy with a side of complicated, and while her heart was full, her mind reeled.

What if things got screwed up...hell, what if she screwed up and drove Hadley away and then she'd lose the one thing more precious to her than anything or anyone else? What if Hadley yearned for another place and needed to go, needed to travel again? Could she handle being apart when they'd just gotten together?

Were they together?

Amelia could feel the lump in her throat begin to swell, threatening to choke off her air and drive her into an anxiety spiral. She couldn't do that; didn't want to leave Hadley alone in her bed. Didn't want to freak herself or Hadley out.

With slow, steady breaths, Amelia eventually got her heart to stop hammering so damn hard. But the itch under her skin was unscratchable. Maybe she could sneak off and go make tea, come back to a sleep-warmed, none the wiser Hadley. Maybe that would calm her in a way no deep breathing could. Movement, action, no matter how small, usually quieted the demons. Because when her demons were incredibly loud and too close and clawing at the walls, and her pain was too much and she wondered if she'd ever be able to move again? Moving helped. Even if it was to shuffle to the kitchen to eat an apple over the sink.

Carefully, Amelia slid her foot out of the covers. The cold air of the room was bracing; winter hadn't yet relinquished its white-knuckle grip. She tensed her arms, gearing up to move as carefully as possible.

"Mmm."

Oh shit.

"Shhh," she said as she reached up to run the backs of her fingers over Hadley's cheek. Gods, the warmth of her skin, the smell of her ....Amelia didn't want to move. But she needed to.

"Ames." Hadley's word (her name, her *name* on Hadley's lips like this, the joy of it, even slurred so) was soft, hush-dark and round.

"It's okay. I'm just making tea."

"Mmmph. Go w'th you?"

"If you want." Amelia smiled. "But you have to get out of bed and it's cold."

"S'fine. Fire."

"We do have a fireplace."

"Yep."

She let Hadley hear her throaty chuckle, feel her fingers pressing into limp hands. "I'll go and turn on the fireplace."

"I'm coming."

Slowly, Hadley dragged herself from bed, half hanging off Amelia, half tangled in the myriad of blankets. But she came, shadowing Amelia's footsteps and dragging her storm quilt along. If Amelia turned around now and saw, she'd bundle them both back into bed and very likely do something incredibly rash.

Because the feel of Hadley's warm skin and the scent of her, dew-dropped jasmine and clean cotton, made something needy wake from its long hibernation. And now wasn't that time.

Hadley curled up in a corner of the big couch by the fireplace, dark eyes watching Amelia as she moved around the kitchen. Making tea was good. It was a focus, a singular dot on the line of routine she knew well. The soundtrack of gentle rain on the old cottage, of the electric flames licking the inside of the protective glass of the fireplace, of Hadley shifting and sighing, made her brain slow down.

The tea was done. Hadley was half asleep by the fire. The rain dropped on the roof over their heads. The ache in her hands from the humidity didn't matter. The lack of sleep didn't matter. All Amelia cared about and knew was Hadley.

They drank their tea in silence after Hadley made sure Amelia was properly under the blanket. Amelia let the cinnamon curl on her tongue, shaking her senses awake as everything around her gently crooned a song of sleep, but desire still thrummed through her.

Then their cups were empty and the silence blossomed around them.

"Hey."

"Hey." Amelia shifted until she could look at Hadley straight on. "Feeling better? I think the storm's moved on."

"Yeah. It's nice now. The rain and the fire." Amelia tracked the hard movement of Hadley's throat. She wanted to put her lips there, then open them so her tongue might discover if Hadley's skin tasted the way it did in her dreams. "You."

Without needing to ask for permission, Hadley's feet, then her legs, became tangled with Amelia's. The physical closeness was nice; more than, actually, because everything felt charged between them now. Their skin electrified, the air between them tense and ready. Waiting.

"This *the talk* then?"

Amelia yanked her head up and gave Hadley a feeble grin. "We're going against the norms, since we just confessed to each other in bed. Before uh..." Her words fumbled on a tongue that suddenly felt like a lead weight in her mouth. "Anything else."

That got Hadley to smile, to shift closer. If Amelia leaned back, she could take Hadley with her. The two of them cradled together in a sweet, aching sort of way that would make her very core clench in anticipation. It was a scary thing to offer, with open arms and expectation on her face, but she did it anyway. And her sweetest, dearest, oldest friend immediately snuggled close, resting her forehead against Amelia's cheek while Hadley's body became a gentle curve in her arms.

"I love you," Amelia said with barely any tremble in her voice. "I love you so much and I don't know when it started -"

"We were eight. And your hair was in pigtails and we were out on the sidewalk between our houses. I saw your hair and your bright blue shirt and all your freckles and I fell in love."

"Oh."

It was Hadley's turn to laugh. "Yeah." She touched Amelia's cheek, fingertips feather-light on her skin. "What about you?"

"I can't compete with that."

"It's not a competition."

"No. But I don't remember the exact moment. Just...*a* moment. Maybe they're the same thing."

"Maybe." Hadley was even closer now, a soft weight in her arms and Amelia wanted to never let go. "But tell me anyway."

Amelia told her. About how they came out of class and headed to their lockers and someone bumped into Hadley, spilling the books from her arms. The heavy crowd around them became a swarm as she and Hadley scrambled to pick everything up. When Amelia handed Hadley the last book, something came over her. Some deep-seated desire, woven through with hormones and familiarity, that made her want to pull a move from a teenage rom-com and press her best friend into the lockers and kiss her.

"I couldn't shake that feeling. Something in me had known for a while but for whatever reason..." Amelia trailed off, watching Hadley's smile grow brighter and brighter. "What?"

"You."

She tried not to wrinkle her nose, focusing instead on the feel of Hadley's hand in hers. "Besides," she said, her tone playfully miffed. "You're the only one who can put up with me."

"I'll take it. All of it. Anything." Hadley tipped her chin up. Offering. So perfectly present and silently asking.

Amelia could never tell her no.

They kissed and kissed and with every little touch and quiet sigh, Amelia could feel something peaceful - something *right* - settle deep in her bones.

CHAPTER EIGHT

*O*ne week to opening

At some point, time became a barrier, a wall, meant to be the ultimate obstacle to their goal. The staff was trained, the wine stocked, their marketing was spreading word of the opening weekend far and wide. But it felt so much like trying to scale a height with no ropes.

The anticipatory energy for the opening had gone from a slight buzz to a full, busy drone. Eager wine lovers and looky-loos stopped by, peeking in the windows. Sometimes yanking on the door as if determination alone would open the chardonnay and cab sav floodgates for them.

Admittedly, Amelia was a genius at catering to the right crowds, using the right words and images. The store's social media climbed the ranks quickly and Hadley took over monitoring comments while Amelia fussed with stock lists and the cash points. Her best friend was good at *enticement* but never realized how integral her own role was in such theater. How could anyone not flock to Amelia's friendly consignment? Her knowledge, her particular brand of charm? It's not as though Hadley could stay away.

Given the number of times over the last week Hadley had put her hands on Amelia's hips or her arm, brushed a kiss over that soft cheek when no one was looking? No, Hadley could never stay away. Especially not since they now spent every night in one bed or the other, curled together under the weight of quilts and content to listen to night settle around them as she and Amelia and the cottage breathed in sync. They never did more than kiss with the occasional gentle touch to an arm or leg. Amelia liked cradling Hadley's face between her hands and drawing their lips together in a slow, even glide that made Hadley's head spin pleasantly.

But she *ached*, and from the way Amelia moved into her touches of late...well. Anticipation was nice but Hadley wanted more. First up, an actual discussion, the one that they'd been avoiding while they raced against time to get Classy Corks ready. It was like being pulled in several directions, strung tight like taffy but ready to snap at any moment. The days blurred by, and at night they fell into bed, body and soul weary.

"We need to talk."

Hadley whipped her head up so fast it made spots dance before her eyes. The tarot reading table jostled. "What?"

Amelia slipped into the seat across from Hadley and leaned forward, right hand cupping her chin. Her pretty brown gaze cut down to the various decks Hadley had been sorting through. "I think we kind of...fell into this. Because it was easy and we'd both wanted it for so long and I just need to even things out." Those eyes were on her now, hot and sharp. "I feel unbalanced, Hads. And I don't want that with you. I want to make sure we're okay and we talk about what we...what we..."

"What we want." She could barely force the words up out of her throat but now they hung in the air on a whisper. They were alone on the second floor, as Larsen and Sara finished up for the night on the main floor and the other staff had long ago left. But it felt like her whisper echoed all around them. "Fuck, Ames, I know. I know we're so busy but I also want to know where we go from here." She touched

Amelia's hand, then squeezed it; got a squeeze in return. "Cause I feel like I've loved you for so long and now it feels so easy, too. But there are things I want and I don't want you to feel like I need them in order to stay by your side. I don't. Ever."

Amelia was quiet for a moment, her stare fixed on their joined hands. "If I'm going to be with anyone, it's you."

Hadley could barely stand it. The desperate beating of her heart kicked up and she could feel the air between them crackle. She was the wild, carefree one, bouncing all over the world and stealing into different beds of women who captured her fancy. But a lot of that wild, reckless energy had faded over the last few years. Maybe it was because she'd started to understand how precious Amelia was, or maybe all that bed-hopping simply lost its luster and excitement. Amelia, in her very typical way, was more methodical, more logical in her approach to relationships. There had been a few, early on, that had made something in Hadley practically *boil* with jealousy, but she'd been the good friend, the supportive person Amelia could call and grouse with and help nurse her broken heart through the telephone line. But her dearest didn't get physical with just anyone. There needed to be real spark, real connection.

And Hadley was certain — quietly, beautifully so, in this very moment and so many others over decades — that she would give Amelia anything. Everything. If all they did was kiss and touch and fall asleep beside each other every night, that was more than enough. Those old notions of sex being the only way to connect with someone on a physical level had long been dashed aside in favor of her bed smelling like Amelia; of oak racks and fresh green things growing in damp soil and the shampoo they now shared.

"You want to be with me?" Hadley leaned forward, inching her way closer; tugging Amelia closer.

Amelia's smile could have snapped her in half. "Only you. Maybe I'm old fashioned. I'm not built for anything other than slow and steady, with one person." The smile turned into a playful smirk and the thing coiling in Hadley's gut tightened. "But I also know that you'll be gentle with me."

The implication in Amelia's words hit like a slow-motion highway pile up. "Oh."

"That's all you can say?"

"Now you're just teasing me."

"I am." Amelia slid her hand over Hadley's. "Should I stop?"

"Nooo, no, no, please don't."

"Night, you two!" Larsen's voice echoed from downstairs. Sara's similar call also filtered up to them. She and Amelia grinned at each other before saying their goodbyes for the day.

And then they were alone somewhere that wasn't the cottage.

Hadley pulled Amelia to her feet, pulled her close, and whispered, "I'll be whatever you want me to with you."

"I know." Amelia cupped her face and pressed their foreheads together. "Let's get takeout and go home."

Hadley gave a fake gasp as they stood. "Who are you and what did you do with my best -"

The kiss cut her off. Hadley melted against Amelia, leaning into her, pressing her fingers into Amelia's back and getting the soft groan she knew the touch would elicit. This last week of cuddling and kisses had been so sweet; sweet enough to twist her heart in new, pleasurable ways. But now Amelia's mouth moved against her own with intent and there was a hand on the back of her neck. A tongue swiping at her bottom lip, leaving Hadley gasping. "Kiss me," Amelia said between short, sharp pecks to her mouth. "Please." Another flicker of tongue. Amelia teasing her.

The always-simmering fire in her for this woman roared to life. Hadley caved. She carefully steered them toward the bit of bare brick wall at the right edge of the bar. It was in full view of anyone pressing close to the storefront's glass window, but she didn't *care*. Amelia didn't either, not with the way her touches turned into clutching, grasping bites of fingertips against Hadley's skin.

Just before Amelia's back hit the wall, Hadley slipped around her to press herself into that space instead. Understanding flickered in Amelia's eyes, something she caught sight of for only a moment before her friend (her best friend, her one and only love) descended on her.

This was a kiss. Maybe *the* kiss that would stoke them both to a flashing roar of fire and need. It certainly left Hadley's head spinning. *Amelia's tongue in her mouth, their bodies pressed so tightly together. The way Amelia leaned into her. The heat of her and the kiss. Soft red hair against her face, making her shiver. Fingertips playing at the buttoned shawl collar of her sweater, as if Amelia wanted to unwrap her from her clothes.*

"Take me home," she groaned against that soft set of lips. "Ames. Please."

Hadley would forever deny that Amelia let out a small whimper, but it was difficult to not grin. Her stoic, beautiful best friend, reduced to a shivery gasp by a few kisses. "Let's go."

Their takeout went cold on the kitchen counter.

Hadley was warm underneath her, arching, moaning, gasping as Amelia kissed her throat and threaded their fingers together. They both shed their heavier outer layers, and as the bedroom fireplace crackled and sputtered, Hadley was right there. Her firm, almost too hot hands rubbing Amelia's bare arms, fingers dipping under the sleeves of her thin t-shirt. She closed her eyes and let herself *feel*. And then her brain got in the way. Wondering, worrying, mildly freaking out over the fact that this was happening *at all*.

"Hey."

Those same warm hands cupped her face and when Amelia looked down at Hadley, she swore she was staring into the sun. Hadley's hair was fanned out around her, waves of dark and lighter browns still echoing with the red highlights she'd put in months ago. "Hey."

Hadley wrinkled her nose. "Where'd you go, babe?"

"Nowhere." Amelia sighed before flopping onto the bed and scooting close to Hadley. "Somewhere. You know me."

A finger gently tapped her temple. "Overthinking."

"Always."

"Mmm. Just means you need a *really* good distraction."

That flirty tone was back in Hadley's voice, but it carried with it a simmering heat. "Are you volunteering?"

"Goddamn right I am." Then Hadley was scrambling over her, pulling Amelia up with easy touches until Amelia's back was against the pillows and Hadley was in her lap. "Let's start here." And she whipped her shirt off. "Tada."

Amelia's eyes didn't know where to go first. Hadley's beautiful skin was bared before her, glowing softly in the dimmed lamplight and orange haze of the fire. The spray of tattooed ivy that curled over her right shoulder, from the very top and down, spilling down to swoop up, near the wings of delicate collarbones. The faded appendectomy scar. The pale, slightly zigzagging stretch marks across her waist. Only Hadley's bra and jeans hiding the rest of her.

And gods, she wanted to touch but Amelia kept her hands on Hadley's hips. "I...can I..."

"God. Yes. *Please*."

But she hesitated. This line, this fuzzy, strange vibrant thing that had always kept them apart *just enough*... Very gently, Hadley put her hands on Amelia's and drew them up. Together. Up over the soft skin of Hadley's belly, pressing carefully. Her head felt too full, it was too much and yet oh so perfect.

"Like this."

Higher they went. Together. Always together.

That touch to Hadley's covered breasts broke the damn, erased the line. Their gazes locked. Amelia's hands shaking. Hadley's breathing quickening. "It's okay," Hadley whispered. "At our own pace. I know you'll take care of me."

Her throat was going to close up, from joy or tears or a bit of fear or all of that together.

Together. They're together. Hadley's not going anywhere.

Touch her. She wants you to.

Hadley's sigh at her touch was something Amelia would never forget. She worried she was too gentle, skittish even, but Hadley's hands were there. Holding her close, showing Amelia how to touch her. How easy it was to drag out a moan from between Hadley's pretty lips with the brush of a thumb, or the slide of fingertips down her sternum. More than once, Hadley pulled her into a kiss, tongue teasing hers. Setting her blood on fire.

And when Hadley yanked Amelia's shirt up, then off, tossing it to the floor, she became something new. Part slinky daydream of lust-hazed eyes and kiss-swollen lips, and part pure *Hadley*. Her soft skin and thick hair and every bit the person she'd always loved. From the time they were eight and playing hopscotch to giggling sixteen year olds swiping wine from the basement bar to go drink in the woods to now. Together in an old cottage outside of the town that had become home.

Amelia watched Hadley shiver under her touch and wanted. How she wanted *everything*, all of it, right now. The next few moments became a blur of sensation, her brain trying to separate the feel of Hadley's lips on her neck from the fingers skimming down her sides. She felt glorious, untethered, and yet so warm she might burn up from the inside out.

"You're so beautiful." Hadley's whisper against her belly, the way she slipped down Amelia's body like she'd done it a hundred, a thousand times. "Ames. God."

"Please come here."

Hadley was so careful, mindful of the pointy bits on her body, as she crawled over Amelia. She knew an errant elbow or knee might hurt and that constant care, as if it were nothing but normal, made her heart swell to the point of aching. "I love you," she said between slick, hot kisses, ones that melded with gentle touches that made her gasp.

Hadley groaned sweetly, kissed her again, then held Amelia's face between her hands. "You are the only person in the world I would do anything for."

"I know."

"Good." Amelia loved Hadley's little knowing smirk, traced the corner of it with her thumb. "Gonna let me stay here tonight?"

She couldn't resist teasing. "No, I figured I'd make out with you and kick you back to your bed-"

Hadley swooped down, laughing, rolling them until her fingers were hooked behind Amelia's head so she could be pulled up into another kiss.

She crushed Hadley to her, got a knee between slim thighs, and let her touch wander. It was good and right and perfect. On their own time, at their own pace. They could be gentle now, and save everything else for later.

CHAPTER NINE

O^{*pening Day*}

O Organized chaos.

Mild panic.

A little bit of worry.

But Amelia felt *good*.

This was it. Already there were eager people outside Classy Corks, satisfied for now with the limited wine tasting Larsen and Hadley were doing at the bistro tables that marched in a curving line around the sidewalk. Those folks had paid upfront for those seats, and while Amelia had worried it would make other customers think the store was too "uppity" for an eclectic town like Breakwater, Hadley and Larsen had been very certain of the opposite. So she let them run with it, while she and Sara and the rest of the staff made sure everything was perfect inside.

Main floor: as picture perfect as humanly possible. Everyone wore their Classy Corks aprons, dark purple with green and white lettering. Each staff member got to pick their apron pattern, so there were paisleys and feather prints running around, as well as a few more interesting choices like polka dots or leopard spots. Amelia kept her apron plain; easier to spot amidst the joyous clashing patterns. Everyone knew the schedule down to a T. The overhead pendant lamps glinted, the tables and shelves were polished, the wine bottles perfectly racked. The art on the walls, courtesy of Hadley's intensely detailed vision, varied from antlers hanging in open picture frames to dried flowers and herbs and strange little baubles that drew the eye. Crystals, oil prints, framed tarot cards with gold and silver foil. Amelia drew the line at macrame, lest the place become too much a draw by those seeking social media clout while posing with goofy faces. It would happen anyways, but she didn't want to lean too hard into a certain aesthetic.

She went upstairs to quadruple-check the Winebrary. It was fully stocked as well and the bar gleamed under the glass and wicker lights. With any luck, a few collectors or high rollers would want to pursue the second floor store room as well, where the highest priced bottles were kept. Amelia didn't want to cater only to that crowd, but in her experience, there were always a handful of people who considered themselves wine connoisseurs, and forgetting to serve them could make or break a business like hers.

Meanwhile, the plant wall she'd had installed (custom, pricey, worth every damn cent) nearly groaned under all the trailing vines, spikes of dark purple or bright pink, and the furls and thorns of various cacti and succulents. The skylight in the ceiling provided ample indirect light and the multi-hued glass cubes in which the plants were nestled glistened like gems. If you looked hard enough, you could make out the subtle lines from where the glassblowers melded together several bits of different reclaimed glass vessels. She hoped customers would ask about the installation and had business cards for the glassblower ready to hand out.

"Hey, Ames?"

Amelia peered over the railing and saw Hadley's grin, bright eyes, hair piled high in a curly mass. Her heart thumped in her chest. Burgeoning, bursting with joy. "Yeah?"

Hadley held up an empty bottle. "We're gonna need more pinot."

"A lot more!" Larsen yelled from the front, and cheer went up from the crowd.

Elation was a thing she hadn't felt in so very long. And now, it threatened to split every seam, every wall she'd ever built. "On it!" Amelia replied as she hurried down the stairs.

"C'mere."

Hadley snagged Amelia by the arm and pulled her into the office. She'd been waiting for Ames to pass by; mostly to hand off another registration sheet full of names and email addresses of those interested in having private parties in the wWnebrary. It was a service they offered, but Hadley had never seen so much interest be flung about so quickly. It was wonderful, and mildly terrifying. And the last thing she wanted to do was overwhelm Amelia on a night where they were all feeling a little that way.

Amelia turned into her embrace with ease, but Hadley could feel her shoulder muscles bunching up. "Hey."

"Hey." She rubbed her palms down the middle of Amelia's back. "It's been wild, yeah?"

"Incredibly so." Amelia rested her forehead against Hadley's and sighed. "One more hour."

"We can do this. And hey..." She kissed Amelia's cheek, then the corner of her mouth. "We'll go home, collapse, and have the morning to relax before this place opens. And I'll give you a backrub and then..." Hadley let her hands drift down Amelia's back, coming to rest just above an ass she wanted to squeeze. "Whatever you want, babe."

Amelia gave a choked laugh, as if she were half scandalized and half willing to do whatever Hadley wanted. "I'm torn between wanting to sleep for a week, and riding high on the adrenaline of the night."

Hadley gave her a grin, a winning one she hoped. "You mean the *success* of the night. Because that's what it is, big time."

"Yeah?"

"Of course, you utter goober." She placed a kiss on one cheek, then the other, and felt the pull of Amelia's smile under her lips. "Let's go finish it out right."

It was tough to keep her energy up as the last hour flew by. It seemed like every time they handed off a check to a table or cashed someone out at the registers, five more people were in line or ready to hand over a credit card for their bill. And at midnight, the shop was still thrumming with people and energy. Breakwater really knew how to turn out a party.

Bit by bit, she sent staff home and for the most part, customers seemed to get the message. There were a few stubborn holdouts, but Amelia was sweet as pie with them, asking if they needed their bill amended and recommending that the bottles they purchased be enjoyed "at home, in your own comforts." Hadley saw one middle aged couple exchange a look before guilt crossed their expressions. She had to duck behind the main counter to keep from laughing.

Her body screamed for sleep, but she wasn't leaving unless Amelia was with her and the shop was doused in darkness, doors locked and the alarms set. Classy Corks was Amelia's, but Amelia was hers. *Finally*. And Hadley wouldn't go anywhere without her. Ever again.

When silence finally cloaked the building, she pulled an exhausted Amelia in close. "How are you feeling, besides drained?"

Amelia chewed on her cheek, her grip on Hadley's waist tight. "Good," she said after a moment. "I don't think I've processed it yet."

"That is more than understandable."

"And yet..." Amelia sighed and looked around. "It's here. It's done. And now we can move forward."

Her heart couldn't take much more tonight. Hadley felt as though she might burst from the sheer joy of it. "We?"

"We. Us." Amelia's kiss was warm and soft. Hadley wanted to melt into the floor. "We did this."

CHAPTER TEN

Nine days later

The shop being closed didn't mean there was no work. They both knew it, but pulling a grousing Hadley out of bed on Monday only succeeded when Amelia waved a mug of coffee under her nose. Thankfully, it was a simple restock and wouldn't take more than a few hours.

Amelia went through her online inventory while Hadley stumbled around. She had to laugh at the way it would look to the outside. The uptight taskmaster with a softer side and the wild child jack-of-all-trades who kept things fun.

Reality was almost always more nuanced.

There was her, the detail-oriented business owner, head down over a gleaming laptop while steam curled off a coffee cup by her elbow, while she worried over a shipment that went missing. Worried about her staff, her customers. And there was Hadley dashing through the halls, bare feet smacking on worn floor boards while a toothbrush dangled from her mouth. The one with the big heart and a smile, but one with an eye for body language and tone, a naturally spiritual person who connected with people on a deeper level. And in truth, Hadley had been far more composed of the two of them over the last week when it came to the store floor.

When two staff members were rather late for the Friday night shift, Hadley kept the staff moving. That instinct to think on her feet also got Larsen doing tastings of a wine that had just come in (one Amelia had yet to taste, but the risk was worth it to keep customers happy around their delays). If a customer was rude, Hadley handled it. If someone wanted to book out the Winebrary, she took care of it with Sara's assistance.

And while Hadley managed the front of the house, Amelia was on the phone, trying to check on the Friday night staff who had gone MIA. They were fine, thankfully and managed to get to work, but she made sure they were settled before sending them out. Then their online shop had received so much traffic, it crashed. A crate of reserved, higher end wines was dropped by the delivery driver. She kept them on time, Hadley kept them motivated. Everything moved in sync.

But lying next to Hadley after cuddling and kissing was starting to make Amelia wonder. They'd been intimate, but only to a certain level; it was hard to find the energy for much after long days in the shop. But that night of the storm lingered in Amelia's memory; the line they'd almost erased but had pulled back from, for the sake of each other. Amelia had kissed Hadley until she was pink in the cheeks and breathless while their hands wandered. But nothing past that. And while her head rattled around with *maybes*, her heart was full. Because having Hadley in any way was more than enough.

Now she needed to not be such a chickenshit and actually speak up for once. She never had any problems before. This was just...too *close* to something like yawning void of doubt. Amelia hated it.

So when she heard Hadley approach the kitchen a few minutes later, looking ready to go for the day and smiling ear to ear, she handed over a cup of coffee and said, "Hey, you."

"Hey." Hadley brushed a kiss over her lips then immediately downed half the cup. "You look more pensive than normal. You okay?"

Amelia patted the stool next to her. "Can we talk for a second?"

No worry crossed Hadley's face, thank god, because Amelia would have rushed to reassure her. The thread of the conversation would have gotten lost and then she'd be scared and frustrated all over again. That was no way to communicate. Hadley was her best friend, her *one*. They could get through anything. "Yeah, what's up?"

Amelia had gone over this in her head dozens of times. Lost precious sleep over it; times during which she had to force herself to not stare at Hadley, as if her mind still wasn't certain this had all happened. Them. *Together*.

She took Hadley's hand in hers and said, "I am not fishing for anything here. I want you to know that. And what we have makes me so happy. But I feel like we should have talked about the more...physical side of things. Maybe sooner. Because I don't want either of us to have expectations and those get all mired in doubt or -"

"Ames."

"Yeah?" Fuck, her heart was pounding so hard.

But nothing on Hadley's face screamed of fear or confusion. Just gentle reassurance and *love*. "You want to talk about sex."

Relief made her deflated "I can't believe I didn't just say that."

Hadley laughed. "I can. I love you, babe, but *buttoned-up* is high up on the list of personality traits for you. Can I help ease the way a bit?"

Hadley waggled her eyebrows for emphasis and Amelia chuckled. "Yes, please. God, I'm going to be embarrassed forever now."

"You don't need to be, but I get it." Hadley pulled Amelia's hand up until she could place a kiss on the inside of her wrist. That little touch set Amelia's nerves on fire. Something flickered to life in Hadley's eyes as she kissed Amelia's wrist again. "We can have as much sex or as little as you want. If you don't want to do that, it would never send me screaming for the hills. Being with you is what I want." Another kiss and now Amelia shivered. "A lot of people discover something new about their partner the first time they have sex. You and me are spiritual, Ames. We don't *need* it, is what I'm saying. But if you *want* it...." She locked eyes with Amelia and placed a final kiss inside her elbow. Amelia thought she might melt. "I'm ready to learn."

Amelia's hesitations and fears crumbled into dust.

Hadley was *right there*, alive and warm and so beautiful and she couldn't stand it any longer. Amelia slid off her stool, their joined hands bringing Hadley with her. She was grinning, so wide it stretched the corners of her mouth. "Okay. Me too."

"You too..." Hadley's little smirk teased the way her tone of voice did, and it only made Amelia's stomach twist itself into more knots, but from the good kind of anticipation now. She stepped forward slowly, her hands on Hadley's shoulders, and steered them to the opposite wall. "So forceful, Ms. de Ville. However will I hold up to your many, *many* charms?"

Amelia wouldn't even grumble about the pain later. It was worth the look on Hadley's face when Amelia cupped her ass and lifted her, forcing Hadley to wrap her legs around Amelia's waist. Hadley laughed, the sound short and startled, before drawing Amelia up into a kiss, her hands so soft along Amelia's jaw. "I don't think you can," Amelia purred back, watching with satisfaction as the tips of Hadley's ears turned pink.

"No, I definitely think I'm weak to you."

"Mmmm." Gently, Amelia bumped Hadley's back into the wall, earning a gasp, and she moved forward even more. Pressed into Hadley's warmth, surrounded by the scent of jasmine and coffee,

Amelia kissed her hard. Desperate. Needing more than what they'd done and now that she knew Hadley wanted something more physical, too, desire chased relief and they ran rampant through her.

The beckoning call of the store could wait.

As daring as Amelia felt, Hadley was the one to tug them down to the bed they now shared. The morning light was filtered through half-shuttered blinds, streaking the dark red sheets with thin lines of soft yellow. That light filtered through the brown and copper of Hadley's hair as she flopped down and pulled Amelia with her. Hadley looked like some kind of nymph, artfully sprawled out as she waited for her lover. It made Amelia shiver, that sight.

"I'm assuming now is okay?" Hadley murmured as Amelia crawled up to lay beside her.

Amelia tangled her fingers through Hadley's hair, watching the light dance through it. "We wouldn't be here if it wasn't."

"Naughty. I like it." Hadley's face was practically cherubic as she grinned. "My, my. Amelia's forgoing work for a little hanky-panky."

"Eugh, don't call it that."

"What should I call it?" Her eyes flashed and her grin shifted, the edge of it turning wicked. "Playing hooky? Morning delight?"

"More like..." Amelia took the moment to skim her palm up Hadley's stomach, stopping only to rest between her breasts. She wanted to feel Hadley's breath hitch as she said, "Me watching you fall apart under my fingers and tongue."

Amelia got her sought-after gasp, and the delectable sight of Hadley biting her lip. "Jesus Christ, Ames. C'mere."

Hadley pulled on her arm until Amelia acquiesced, sliding on top of Hadley so she could rest between strong, slim thighs and work on shoving Hadley's dark blue sweater out of the way. "You've seen that already," Hadley teased in a throaty whisper as Amelia pushed the sweater up higher.

"I have, but that doesn't mean I don't want to now." Amelia helped Hadley wiggle out of the sweater, taking a moment to pull back and really look. Hadley's tawny, freckled shoulders sloped gently down to long, wiry arms. She'd always been willowy but Amelia loved how ethereal she looked right now in the thin sunlight. Hadley practically sparkled, glimmering with energy and life. And as badly as Amelia *wanted*, she also needed to remember this. The glow, the light. Hadley's expectant, warm smile. The way her hair fanned out across their bed.

"I like it when you stare at me like that."

"Like what?"

Hadley shrugged. "Like you're trying to burn the moment into your mind. It makes me feel..." She blinked, turned away.

"Hads."

Hadley swallowed hard and turned back. "Special. You always make me feel special."

With a groan, Amelia collapsed on her, pressing kisses to Hadley's jaw and neck, loving the way Hadley squirmed in delight. Soft gasps filled the quiet air and they wrenched Amelia's heart in different directions, forcing her to bounce between tenderness and lust, adoration and love and everything else Hadley evoked within her.

Nimble fingers worked their way down her shirt, the barest brush of fingertips making her shiver. When Hadley shoved at the plaid in an attempt to push it down her shoulders, Amelia straightened only to shrug it off and peel out of her bralette.

"I wanted to do that," Hadley pouted, but her eyes were fixed on Amelia's breasts. She felt a surge of confidence; it was a hell of an ego boost to be stared at in such a way. Like Hadley wanted all of it, everything, all of her...*right now.*

"Should we..." Hadley swallowed hard, dropped her voice. "Go slow, I'm guessing?"

Trying not to grin, Amelia settled on the bed beside her and ran her touch over Hadley's belly. Her skin was so soft and the very air around them was perfumed with jasmine. "You could lay right here and let me take care of you," she whispered into Hadley's neck while hooking her fingers into the waistband of Hadley's jeans. "Doesn't mean you can't participate, but I enjoy this."

"Taking care of me?" Hadley's voice was thin, shaky at the edges.

"Like you do for me. I want to repay -"

"Ames." Hadley turned to look at her, all levity gone from her expression. "What I want is you. There's no *repayment.* Not for being my friend." She brushed the hair out of Amelia's face, the touch so delicate it made Amelia shiver. "Or my partner."

The tears welled up in her eyes so quickly Amelia didn't have the chance to blink them out of existence. All she could do was nod and kiss Hadley and hold her close until they were both panting. "I wasn't trying to make you cry," Hadley said against her mouth.

Surely not all of those tears were hers. "I wasn't trying to make you cry, either."

Hadley pulled back to show Amelia her tear-stained face and soft smile. Amelia's heart melted. "Haven't even gotten each other naked and we're both a mess," Hadley said between laughs. "Oh my god."

Amelia shook her head with a laugh. This morning had absolutely not gone the way she'd expected. She loved it, every ridiculous moment and every tear and every single kiss she got to keep close to her heart. "Let me take care of you," she whispered, slipping down Hadley's body to pop the button on her jeans. "Please."

Hadley nodded while the sunlight danced across her body. Amelia couldn't have asked for a better moment, a better *yes*. But Hadley naked was a glorious thing, all soft skin and long limbs and dips and valleys and curves and old scars from falling out of trees or off bicycles. Amelia remembered a lot of them and set about pressing her lips to every single one.

Hadley tipped her head back and sighed as Amelia kissed her way across all those memories. The hands in her hair were gentle, reverent. And every time Hadley squirmed in delight or shied away out of sensitivity, Amelia remembered. A new set of memories to catalog with the old, but all of them making up the things that were her. Them. *Together.*

One month later

"Why, Mr. Buttons! Look at you in that snazzy vest." Hadley grinned as the giant ball of fluff and gravelly meows padded up to her. He was wearing a dark green corduroy vest with glinting brass buttons and she knew she hadn't made that one. Hadley leaned down to peer at the garment and saw a few wonky stitches, a few places where the seam had been started and stopped, as if made by a slightly hesitant hand. "Did Amelia make you this?"

Mr. Buttons meowed then turned tail and padded through the open back fence. That's when Hadley heard it. *Music*. Strains of soft jazz floating on the cool spring air, followed by the *pop* of a wine cork. It was a sound Hadley could probably mimic on cue, as much as she heard it day in and day out.

Amelia *had* left the store early to pick up an order of glassware, leaving Hadley in charge with a swift kiss behind the counter and a wave to the rest of the staff. Yes, Hadley's birthday wasn't until the weekend and they had dinner reservations at a French fusion place a few towns over. But leave it to Amelia to do something else, prepare some token of affection unprovoked and as a complete surprise.

Hadley followed Mr. Buttons into the backyard, where early spring greenery popped out of the ground and the lacey leaves of tulips pushed up against already-blossoming crocus. And there on their little patio was Amelia. Her hair was piled into a messy bun, leaving soft tendrils to caress her face. She was wearing a boatneck sweater the color of spun gold with the black jeans Hadley loved so much. And below her collarbone, hanging off a thick silver chain, sat the key Hadley had given her. That sight never failed to make Hadley's heart beat just a little faster.

"For you." Amelia handed Hadley a full glass of red wine and then pulled out one of the chairs. The table was set with steaming bowls of rice and chicken stir fry, which Amelia knew was Hadley's comfort food. Another full bottle of wine sat nearby, as if Amelia anticipated they'd need it. And all around them were flickering candles. Hadley realized most of the candles had come from the cottage, recognizing the various glass and metal holders and hurricane jars. The dancing light made the garden look like something out of a fairy story, and with Mr. Buttons prowling the yard in his new vest, and Amelia looking at her with soft devotion...all of it left her with only one thing to do.

"You're way too good to me," Hadley said before setting both their glasses aside and sweeping Amelia into a kiss. "I love you. I love you so much and I'll never stop saying."

"Please don't," Amelia whispered against her lips. "I love you, too."

When they finally broke apart, Hadley took the moment to rub her thumbs along Amelia's cheeks, just to watch them go pink under her attention. "You are perfect," she said softly, enjoying the way Amelia's gaze went heavy-lidded and dark. "For me. You are perfect for me. I'd like to think somehow we've always known."

"How we fit together?"

"Yeah." She swallowed against the lump in her throat.

"Like a romance book."

That made her laugh delightedly. "Aren't we the perfect book heroines? The best friends who slowly fall in love? Me, the world traveler who could never be pinned down. And you, the beautiful, compassionate, intelligent one who always lures me back."

Amelia frowned. "I think you're downplaying yourself there quite a bit, Hads."

She grinned. "Oh, then do compliment me. I'm all ears."

And as she'd hoped, Amelia decided to play along. She leaned in and kissed Hadley on the forehead, then on the tip of her nose. Her chin. Both her cheeks. And just before Amelia kissed Hadley's lips, she said, "My one and only happily ever after."

Author Thanks

My thanks to Jenny Michelle, Anna Gordon, and Cayla for their early reads, edits, and feedback. They are trusted readers and friends who do so much for me and I cannot expression my appreciation enough for them and their time and energy.

Also By Halli Starling

Wilderwood

Twelfth Moon

Ask Me For Fire

When He Beckons

A Brighter, Darker Art

The Way We Wind

Coup De Coeur (FORTHCOMING 2024)

About the Author

Halli Starling is a queer librarian, reader, gamer, and author.

Halli has always been involved with books, and her love of the written word inspired her to get her MLIS and continue her book career outside of public libraries. When not writing, she co-hosts The Human Exception podcast, plays D&D, and spends time in the beautiful outdoors of Michigan. She is available for podcasts, interviews, panels, and book signings.